T0196849

Sit, Stay, Slay

Books by V.M. Burns

Mystery Bookshop Series
THE PLOT IS MURDER
READ HERRING HUNT
THE NOVEL ART OF MURDER
WED, READ & DEAD
BOOKMARKED FOR MURDER
A TOURIST'S GUIDE TO MURDER

Dog Club Series
IN THE DOG HOUSE
THE PUPPY WHO KNEW TOO MUCH
BARK IF IT'S MURDER
PAW AND ORDER
SIT, STAY, SLAY

Published by Kensington Publishing Corporation

Sit, Stay, Slay

V.M. Burns

LYRICAL UNDERGROUND
Kensington Publishing Corp.
www.kensingtonbooks.com

LYRICAL UNDERGROUND BOOKS are published by

Kensington Publishing Corp.
119 West 40th Street
New York, NY 10018

All Kensington titles, imprints, and distributed lines are available at special quantity discounts for bulk purchases for sales promotion, premiums, fund-raising, educational, or institutional use.

Special book excerpts or customized printings can also be created to fit specific needs. For details, write or phone the office of the Kensington Sales Manager: Kensington Publishing Corp., 119 West 40th Street, New York, NY 10018. Attn. Sales Department. Phone: 1-800-221-2647.

First Electronic Edition: December 2020
ISBN-13: 978-1-5161-0995-1 (ebook)
ISBN-10: 1-5161-0995-3 (ebook)

First Print Edition: March 2020
ISBN-13: 978-1-5161-0996-8
ISBN-10: 1-5161-0996-1

Printed in the United States of America

Acknowledgments

Thank you to John Scognamiglio, Michelle Addo, and everyone from Kensington.

I am so grateful to have a large extended family who have helped me in various ways. I appreciate my work family: Linda Kay, Monica Jill, Tim, Chuck, Lindsey, Kristie, and Sandy. I appreciate my team (past and present): Amber, Derrick, Eric, Jennifer, Robin, and Grace, Deborah, Tena, and Jamie. Thanks to Abby Vandiver, Alexia Gordon, and E.L. Reddick for legal and medical advice, and to Deborah Childs for the great insurance information. Special thanks to my family and to my good friends Shelitha Mckee and Sophia Muckerson.

Chapter 1

"What do you mean you didn't qualify?" My best friend, Scarlet Jefferson—Dixie, to her friends—stared in utter and complete disbelief. Dixie was wearing a beautiful pink sweater with rhinestones, slacks, and black leather boots. At close to six feet tall, she was a Southern belle with Dolly Parton big hair. Despite the fact that we were attending a dog show, she looked as beautifully made up and well dressed as ever.

Pleasantly plump at five foot four and with dark hair and eyes, I was comfortable in jeans, tennis shoes, and an Eastern Tennessee Dog Club T-shirt. Without makeup and my hair pulled back in a ponytail, I felt like a troll next to Dixie.

"I thought we had done well enough to at least qualify." I held my Toy Poodle, Aggie, close to my chest. "I was hoping you noticed what we did wrong."

"You didn't do anything wrong, nothing that should have gotten you disqualified." She took a deep breath and paused. "Aggie lagged a little bit during the heel free exercise, but it wasn't bad. She caught up when you went faster, and she stayed up the entire rest of the time. Apart from a couple of crooked finishes, she was great." She reached over and gave Aggie's ear a scratch.

I should have known this trial wouldn't run smoothly from the first moment I stepped out of my car and saw Dixie and the club president, Lenora Houston, in an intense discussion.

Lenora was an Amazon of a woman with short-cropped white hair. Head up. Shoulders back. Lenora marched around the front of the building like a drill sergeant, which wasn't unusual since she was former military.

However, her lips were moving, and she looked ready to spit bricks, as my friend Monica Jill would say.

I had gotten there just in time to hear Dixie ask, "What's wrong?"

"This is a mock trial. You and all the other judges recognized that and graciously waived your fees." She glared. "All except one."

"Let me guess—Naomi Keller," Dixie said.

Lenora nodded. "She was as sweet as pie when she agreed to judge. Now . . ." She pounded her fist in her hand. "We're only charging five dollars per entry, just enough to cover the expenses of Utility and an extra trash pickup. If we have to pay her, we're going to go in the hole."

Dixie sighed. "Do we have a choice?"

Lenora stared for a few moments. "No."

"Then, as much as I hate to admit it, we're stuck between a rock and a hard place, and we'll just have to pay her."

"I know, but it really burns my butt that she told us she was waiving her fee and now says, 'I changed my mind,' like she's decided to have decaf rather than regular coffee." Lenora turned and marched back inside the building.

On the surface, Dixie had looked as cool and calm as always. Only a close examination revealed the vein pulsing on the side of her head and the hardened look in her eyes.

"Was the lagging enough to disqualify us?" I asked.

"Not at all. It's a few points off. She should have qualified."

The Eastern Tennessee Dog Club (ETDC) owned a building that was crude but functional. It was a long, low building with a metal roof. It wasn't fancy, but it was located on more than three acres of land, which was mostly fenced, and provided a great venue for dog shows. The building also offered tons of parking, another must-have for dog shows and training facilities. Inside, the walls weren't insulated, and the concrete floors were covered in green vinyl mats. The matted area of the room was sectioned off with white, folding, accordion-ring gates that made what looked like a small picket fence. The unmatted area was left for spectators. There wasn't a lot of space for chairs, but the building had a few bleachers, which today were full, and limited space for dog crates along a side wall near the door.

We stood outside of the ring and watched a woman with a large playful St. Bernard puppy.

B.J. Thompson joined our group. "Is this the kiss and cry area?"

"You too?" I asked.

B.J. was Black, with dark skin and hair, which she wore in long braids that trailed down her back. "I don't care what that mean old judge thinks."

She cuddled her white West Highland Terrier. "Mummy wuvs you, and you're going to get that smelly liver treat anyway." She looked up. "I was saving it for a celebration if she qualified, but I think she earned the treat, and I'm giving it to her."

Dixie petted Snoball. "She absolutely earned the liver."

An excellent obedience instructor and judge, Dixie was known for being tough but fair. She believed in a positive approach to dog training, which included lots of positive reinforcement and treats, but not just any treats. She advocated the use of treats that were so special, a dog would sell its soul to get them. These "soul-selling" treats included some of the most foul-smelling dried liver, which Dixie ordered in bulk.

The third woman in Dixie's dog training class, Monica Jill, sauntered over to our group.

"Where's Jac?" I asked.

"In his crate, where he belongs." She folded her arms across her chest. "I am so angry with that dog." She looked from me to B.J. "Did you see what he did?"

Jac was a black dog with a white spot. He was most likely a terrier/ Labrador mix, but you couldn't tell what he was by looking at him. He was a young dog with a lot of energy. Getting him to the point that he was able to compete, even in a mock obedience event, had taken a great deal of practice and patience. He had done surprisingly well in the early part of the trial. He heeled both on and off leash. He stood still while the judge examined him and even did the recall exercise. He lost points during the figure-eight heel pattern when he stopped to sniff the crotch of one of the men who was serving as a post for the figure eight; however, that should have only been a few points off. Jac's disqualification came during the group exercise. When all the owners lined up their dogs against the wall, commanded the dogs to sit and stay, and then walked six feet away, Jac didn't stay. Instead, he followed Monica Jill and was standing there looking up at his owner, tail wagging and big brown eyes full of love and adoration, when she turned around.

"He's still young," Dixie reminded her.

Monica Jill, a tall thin woman with dark hair and dark eyes, wasn't ready to forgive so easily. She pointed to Aggie. "He's older than Aggie."

"You can't always go by age. The breed and sex can play a big part in development and maturity." Dixie smiled. "Aggie's a female and a Toy Poodle. They tend to mature a lot faster than males."

Monica Jill huffed. "Well, he isn't getting any liver treats today."

B.J. and I exchanged glances, which indicated we knew Monica Jill wasn't as tough as she pretended to be. She also wouldn't hold a grudge for more than a few minutes. By the time she went home tonight, we knew Jac would be eating liver, just like Snoball and Aggie.

We became distracted watching the St. Bernard puppy. He bounded around the ring like a small pony, tongue hanging out, a look of pure joy on his face, while his owner walked the heel pattern alone. Eventually, the puppy finished his romp, hiked his leg, and peed on the ring gate.

"At least Jac didn't pee in the ring," B.J. said.

"Soiling the ring is an automatic disqualification, isn't it?" I asked.

Dixie nodded.

We watched as two members of the dog club sprayed and wiped away the soiled area to prevent other dogs from getting distracted and adding their own scents. Having spent an entire day cleaning up at a dog show a few months ago, I was grateful to be competing and not working this event.

The last member of Dixie's obedience class, Dr. Morgan, and his German Shepherd, Max, were next. We watched as they entered the ring and waited for the judge to begin. Dr. Morgan was short and bald, with an egg-shaped head that always reminded me of Agatha Christie's detective, Hercule Poirot.

Both Max and his owner were serious, and they performed their exercises with an intense concentration that bordered on obsession. No smiles cracked their exterior façades. The only hint of levity came from the bright green ETDC T-shirt Dr. Morgan wore over his dress shirt and slacks. The shirts were a gift from Monica Jill for the members of Dixie's class and bore the ETDC logo on the front, with the words Dixie's Pack on the back.

From our vantage point, it looked as though Dr. Morgan and Max would qualify and save our class from total humiliation. When the last exercise was over, we cheered as they walked out of the ring. Within minutes, Dr. Morgan and Max joined our group.

"Good boy, Max." We showered both the dog and owner with praise. Snoball had a crush on the GSD and licked him shamelessly, while Max ignored her and tried to get Aggie's attention.

The club volunteers who were working the table at the edge of the ring took the scoresheets from the judge. They tallied the points for each handler and then recorded them on a whiteboard outside the gate. We waited excitedly until the worker marked DQ beside number 23, which was the number on the armband worn by Dr. Morgan.

We stared in shock at the two letters. I didn't think anything could have been worse until the judge grabbed a large, blue first-place ribbon and turned to face the crowd.

"St. Bernard number twenty-two."

There was a stunned silence in the building. Eventually, the woman with the St. Bernard puppy returned to the ring and received their first-place ribbon.

When I finally found words, I turned to Dixie. "How is that possible? I didn't see anything that would have disqualified Max."

"Neither did I." Dixie glared. "But you can bet your bippy I'm going to find out."

Chapter 2

The confrontation didn't happen immediately. First, the shocked St. Bernard owner and the second- and third-place winners received their ribbons, took pictures with the judge, and cleared the ring. ETDC had a large glass award that the president, Lenora Houston, presented to the judge. The award was supposed to be a token of the club's appreciation, and we'd had it made before Naomi Keller demanded monetary payment for her services. Lenora Houston, with her military buzz cut and rigid physique, looked as though she had just sucked a lemon. She smiled for the pictures, but her smile looked more like a grimace.

During the pictures, Dixie was called to the club's office to take care of a problem with the computer. However, confrontation was inevitable.

"If that woman has any sense of self-preservation," B.J. said, "she'll avoid that office like the plague."

When the pictures were done, we watched Naomi Keller make her way to the office. Monica Jill, B.J., and I exchanged glances.

"We've got to help her," Monica Jill said, looking from the office to the rest of us. "Dixie was loaded for bear. She'll eat that woman alive."

I stared at my friend. "I don't know what that means."

"Yankee." B.J. snorted. "It means, we better get in there and make sure Little-Miss-I'm-going-to-disqualify-your-whole-obedience-class knows that we've got Dixie's back."

Monica Jill stamped her feet. "We are not going back there like some posse intent on intimidation. We are going to keep our friend from strangling that woman."

B.J. grunted.

We took a few steps forward before we realized that Dr. Morgan wasn't following, and we turned around to see that he was shaking his head.

"I work for the county," he said. "I can't get involved in anything that could potentially involve the police."

B.J. walked back to him and shoved Snoball into his arms. "Good, then you can hold our dogs."

I hesitated a split second and then shoved Aggie into his chest and followed my two friends toward the raised voices.

Dixie towered over the shorter woman like a dinosaur. "If you have a problem with me, then be woman enough to confront *me* personally. How dare you penalize my students?"

"I don't think I've ever seen Dixie this mad before," Monica Jill whispered. "I was only half-joking earlier when I said we needed to stop her from killing that judge."

"Well, I wasn't." B.J. pounded her fist in her palm. "They 'bout to throw down. I got twenty dollars that says Dixie takes her out with two punches."

Monica Jill gave B.J. a shove. "This is serious."

B.J. chuckled. "Oh, alright." She turned to me. "You've known Dixie longer than the rest of us. What's the plan?"

I shrugged. "Plan? What plan? I don't have a plan."

B.J. and Monica both stared at me.

"What?"

Monica Jill whispered, "You always have a plan."

After a quarter century of friendship, I could only recall one other time when I'd ever seen Dixie as angry as she was right now. "Wait, what did you say this judge's name was?"

"Naomi Keller," Monica Jill whispered.

Naomi Keller sat in her chair with an innocent *I have no idea what you're talking about look* on her face. However, as Dixie continued to rage about jealousy and bias, a transformation occurred. Naomi Keller's face morphed from human to something animalistic and feral.

"Don't blame me because your little obedience groupies failed to deliver." She smirked. "Dixie's pack."

I heard Monica Jill gasp, and then I glanced down at my bright green T-shirt.

"You can honestly sit there and say you weren't biased when you gave a first-place ribbon to a dog that peed in the ring?"

Someone nudged me and then slid into the office. It was the St. Bernard's handler, and she was carrying the blue ribbon. "Ah-hem." She courageously approached the two fighting women.

Naomi Keller flipped a switch. Instantly, her facial contortions ceased. She plastered on a huge smile, and her voice became syrupy sweet. "Yes, dear. May I help you?"

She pointed at Dixie. "She's right. Bernie peed in the ring. He should have been disqualified."

The smile froze on Naomi's face. "Nonsense. That was purely an accident. He's young and energetic—"

The woman merely shook her head. "Nope. I can't take something I didn't earn. It wouldn't be right." She placed the blue ribbon on the table, turned, and walked out.

Naomi Keller scowled at Dixie. "You see what you did to that poor woman?"

"What I did?"

"If you hadn't made such a fuss, none of this would have happened. It's just a mock show, which doesn't even count, but, as always, you have to be the center of attention." She glanced around at the faces of the crowd that had gathered in the tiny office and gave a chuckle. "Dixie always did think she was the top dog when her skills were never quite up to par."

A flush rose quickly up Dixie's neck, and she balled her hands into fists. "What does this have to do with me and my *skills*?"

"They say, those who can't do . . . teach, and I don't see you entered."

Dixie reached across the table and grabbed a pen and a blank entry form. She scribbled on it and then handed the form to one of the startled women who was working the show. "I'll see you in Utility." The crowd parted like the Red Sea after Moses lifted his staff, and Dixie marched out.

Chapter 3

After a moment of shocked indecision, Monica Jill, B.J., and I quickly recovered and followed our friend. We didn't need to see the interior lights on in the luxury RV that Dixie drove to dog shows to know where she was. Not bothering to knock, we hurried inside.

Dr. Morgan sat at the kitchen table, drinking a cup of coffee. Snoball and Aggie were curled up on the sofa with Max and Leia, one of Dixie's two black Standard Poodles.

My puzzled expression and body language asked the question, but before he could respond, Dixie and Chyna came from the bedroom of the RV.

Dixie's hair was pulled into a ponytail, and we knew she meant business.

"Ah, you got your hair pulled back like you ready for a fight," B.J. joked. "You need me to hold her down while you beat her, or you got this?"

Dixie smiled. "I don't think that'll be necessary, but I appreciate the offer." She pulled out a grooming table. "Chyna, up."

Champion Chyna, 9th Wonder of the World, was a beautiful black Standard Poodle, who had spent a good part of her life on a grooming table while she competed in conformation dog shows, like Westminster and Crufts, and she had a room full of ribbons to prove it. Despite the fact that she was now retired from competition and no longer had the mane, bracelets, or top knot from her glory days, she was well trained and obeyed. On the table, she lay down and settled in for what promised to be the hours of time Dixie would spend perfecting her coat.

"What are you doing?" B.J. asked.

"I'm getting Chyna ready to go into the ring."

We exchanged glances.

I cleared my throat. "I think B.J. meant, *why* are you doing that? You're not showing conformation, and it won't matter if her coat is perfect in the obedience ring or not."

"Before we go into the ring . . . any ring, I always spend some time brushing and grooming my dogs." Dixie brushed Chyna. "It relaxes the dog and helps settle my nerves."

We watched.

"Are you nervous?" Monica Jill asked.

Dixie gave Chyna several long strokes with the slicker brush. "I'm angry, and I'm hoping that doing something familiar, like grooming my dogs, will help me to calm down and remain calm."

We sat and watched. Eventually, Dixie told Chyna to turn over, and she started in on the other side.

"Are you going to tell us about Naomi Keller, or do we have to wait until you finish grooming both dogs?"

Dixie brushed a bit more and then took a deep breath. "Naomi Keller and I went to the same high school, although she was just Naomi Eastlake then. We used to be best friends. We were in 4-H, and we both competed in agility, conformation, and obedience. Sometimes she'd win, and sometimes I'd win." She paused. "But as we got older, things changed. We both went out for the cheerleading team, and we both made it."

Monica Jill raised her hand. "Let me guess—you were head cheerleader?"

Dixie nodded. "Honestly, I wasn't even trying, but something changed after that. I started dating Beau." She paused for a moment, as though remembering, then continued. "He was the captain of the football team."

"Did she have a crush on him?" I asked.

"No. At least I didn't think she did . . . not then, anyway." She sighed. "I have no idea. If she did, she never said anything. In fact, she was dating someone else."

B.J. sipped her coffee. "The captain of the basketball team?"

"How did you know?"

"Girl, Stevie Wonder could have seen that coming."

"Anyway, she became jealous and competitive. Our friendship suffered—"

"I'll bet it did."

Monica Jill swatted at B.J. "Stop interrupting. So, what happened next?"

Dixie took a deep breath. "Not much. We left for college. I went to school in Illinois, and she went to the University of Tennessee."

"With Beau?" I asked.

She nodded. "Beau and I were pretty serious, but I wanted to get out of Tennessee and see the world. The last thing I wanted was to follow him around like some football groupie." She brushed Chyna. "Anyway, Beau and I went through a rough patch and . . . well, she made a move on him."

"The dirty little b—"

"B.J.!" Monica Jill yelled.

B.J. rolled her eyes and sipped her coffee.

Dixie smiled. "Nothing happened. Beau told me everything, and eventually, we made up and got married. When I started competing again, Naomi and I ran into each other at dog shows from time to time, but she showed Greyhounds, and I showed poodles. Poodles show in the Non-Sporting Group and Greyhounds are in the Hound Group. Unless we both made it to Best in Show, we weren't in direct competition, but there was always something . . . whenever we found ourselves at the same shows."

"Something like what?" I asked.

"If I left my RV or my grooming station unattended, something unusual would happen. My clippers or scissors would be missing. Or a dress I brought would suddenly have a tear or every pair of pantyhose would have runs. I can't prove that she did anything, but if we weren't at the same shows, I didn't have those problems."

B.J. frowned. "Sounds fishy to me."

Dixie finished brushing her dog. "Chyna, off."

Chyna stood up, stretched, and yawned as though she'd just worked a double shift at a factory, and then jumped down off the table.

"So, you think she disqualified all of us to get even with you?" Dr. Morgan asked.

"I don't want to think that, but there's no other excuse for how she could qualify a dog that soiled the ring, and I didn't see anything that you and Max did which would merit disqualification."

Dr. Morgan stared down into his cup. "Thank you, but you don't have to do this." He looked around. "Not for us."

"He's right," I said. "It's just a mock trial and doesn't count."

Monica Jill raised her hand. "Jac earned his disqualification fair and square."

Dixie glanced around at each of us. "I know I don't have to, but I want to."

I walked over to Dixie. "Given what she just did, you can't believe she'll give you a fair shot."

She smiled. "Actually, I'm rather hoping she doesn't."

"What?"

Dixie went to a drawer and held up a video camera. She passed it to Dr. Morgan. "Do you know how to use this?"

He took the camera and smiled. "You bet your bippy I do."

B.J. sat up. "Oh, I get it. You're going to have him videotape it, and if she cheats you, then you have evidence to nail her."

Dixie smiled, but it didn't reach her eyes. "I don't want to hurt her. I don't want to hurt anyone, but judges are supposed to operate with integrity. Exhibitors need to be able to trust that we do the right things for the right reasons. Without integrity . . . well, we might as well not even bother."

I hugged Dixie. "Well said."

Monica Jill pulled out her cell phone. "We should all record it."

"I'm in," B.J. said.

"Okay, well, you all better get out of here and let Chyna and me finish our routine." She opened a drawer and took out a small box, which I knew contained her equipment for Utility. "It's been quite a while since Chyna retired from the obedience ring." She glanced down at her dog and smiled. "I hope she remembers how to work."

"She'll remember," I said. "She's got the best instructor on the planet."

We left, leaving our dogs to relax and lounge in the luxury of Dixie's RV and letting Dixie and Chyna practice in peace and quiet.

The East Tennessee Dog Club was sponsoring an official dog trial in two weeks. It would be Aggie and my first obedience competition, and my nerves were in overdrive. In fact, all of the members of Dixie's class were anxious. We wanted to do a good job and make her proud of us. In an effort to help us calm down, Dixie had suggested this mock trial. The idea was to get experience with actual judges and to become familiar with the atmosphere of a real trial. It was supposed to be the balm that soothed our troubled souls. Unfortunately, this experience was having the exact opposite effect.

Naomi Keller wasn't the only judge. In fact, there were two others. When word got around that we were having a mock trial, people sent their entries in droves. Initially, Dixie was going to judge the entire event, but the sheer number of entries required additional help. I found myself wishing we'd never done this.

We went outside to observe some of the trials that were going on behind the building.

I hadn't been competing in dog sports long, but I knew there were three basic classes for obedience: Novice, Open, and Utility. Within each class, there were multiple levels. Dixie's class was at the bottom in Novice A, which meant that we were not only beginners but we had never had a dog achieve the Novice Obedience Title. Novice B was for people who had gotten a Novice title before on a different dog. This meant our group had true beginners.

We walked around and observed Novice B and Open trials and then wandered off, each looking at something that interested us. I stood at the edge of the ring and watched as an older, gray-haired woman and a muscular Rottweiler competed in the exercises for the Open class.

I got a nudge that sent me careening forward. I would have fallen flat on my face if someone hadn't grabbed me. As I turned to thank my savior, I saw a familiar face. "Red."

Dennis Olson, Red to his friends, was five foot ten, stocky and rock solid. He had dark eyes and sandy red hair that he wore in a short buzz cut that screamed former military. He also had a long scar on the right side of his face, which hinted at a dark tale that was often reflected in his eyes.

I smiled. "Thank you."

He pulled me close and kissed me.

"Don't thank me too soon." He glanced down at his dog, Steve Austin, who was a pit bull/Labrador mix who had adopted Red when his owner was murdered. "He goosed you."

I bent down and grabbed the big, droolly dog's cheeks. "Did you do that to me?" I said in the baby talk I used with dogs, which I knew would thoroughly embarrass Red.

Steve Austin's tail wagged faster, which caused his back end to wag. When he couldn't contain it anymore, he lay down on his back, belly exposed, and wiggled his entire body.

Red shook his head. "Come on. Have some dignity."

Steve Austin and I ignored him. I scratched his belly, and the eighty-pound dog lay with his tongue hanging out the side of his mouth.

"We don't care what the grumpy man says, do we?"

The dog, with a look of utter delight, wiggled even more in the grass.

"Great." Red glanced around. "How long is this public humiliation going to last?"

I chuckled, stood up, and linked arms. "I'm glad you came."

"Sorry I'm late, but we got here as quickly as we could. How'd it go?"

"We?" I looked down at the dog.

He shook his head. "No. We." He pointed to a woman standing at a ring nearby, watching a Great Dane.

"Madison. I'm so glad you brought her."

Madison Cooper was a beautiful young woman with long dark hair and dark eyes who we had met a few months ago when she was working at a pet spa. My son, David, took quite a shine to her and learned that Madison had skills as a computer hacker. Fortunately, she was a white-hat hacker who used her powers for good rather than evil, and she now worked with Red at the Tennessee Bureau of Investigation.

I gave Red a rundown on Aggie and my first time in the mock trial competition and our disqualification. Then I gave him a detailed play-by-play of Dixie's altercation with the judge and the upcoming obedience smackdown.

Red shook his head. "This sounds like a recipe for disaster."

"Isn't it exciting?" B.J. said, having sneaked up while I was talking. "It's like the Sharks and the Jets in *West Side Story*."

"What time is this obedience rumble going down?"

I nudged him. "This is serious business."

B.J. clapped. "Dixie is going to mop the floor with that judge, and if she disqualifies her . . ." She cracked her knuckles and took a few jabs in the air like a prize fighter. "Well, then it's on like Donkey Kong."

"It's been a while since Dixie competed," Red said. "You never know."

I stopped walking and stared at him. "What are you saying?"

He shrugged. "I'm just suggesting that you two might want to keep an open mind. If Dixie is disquali—"

"You can stop right there, Mister TBI Officer," B.J. said. "Dixie is going to win, and that's the end of that." She gave him a stare that challenged him to argue the point. Thankfully, Red was smart enough to keep quiet.

We went back inside to make sure we had ringside seats. The trial, which earlier had been poorly attended, was packed. In fact, practically everyone had heard of the argument between Dixie and Naomi Keller and had come to watch the showdown.

We squeezed into the front row and got our cell phones out and pointed them at the ring. Red glanced in my direction several times, and he looked on the verge of speaking, but something held him back. I glanced in his direction. "What's wrong?"

"Nothing. I just need to ask you something."

"Okay, but can it wait? I need to record this."

"Sure." He released a heavy sigh, and I was just about to apologize and give him my full attention when I saw Dixie and Chyna walk into the building.

Naomi Keller was in the ring where Aggie and I had performed earlier. Dixie and Chyna approached the gate entrance, Dixie with her armband and her game face firmly in place.

When instructed, Dixie and Chyna entered the ring and stood at the chalk line. Dixie stood tall and serious, and Chyna was as regal as ever.

I had watched Dixie and Chyna perform various exercises, but today was truly a sight to behold. During the heeling exercises for Utility, Chyna put her right shoulder against Dixie's left leg and performed the exercise as if she were glued to Dixie's side. When Dixie signaled for Chyna to stay and walked away, Chyna didn't move one toenail until Dixie signaled her. Each and every exercise was done to perfection, and the knowledgeable crowd knew it, and struggled to contain themselves from clapping. There were two scent exercises coming up that worried me. Dixie handed the judge her box, which we'd seen in the RV earlier.

"What's that?" Red whispered.

"Dumbbells, but they call them articles."

"Okay, but what's happening?"

Dixie and Chyna turned so their backs were to the ring and waited.

"You have two sets of five dumbbells from two different materials." I glanced at him to see if he was following. "The materials are wood, metal, or leather. Dixie has metal and leather. So five metal and five leather. You with me?"

He nodded.

"Dixie will be asked to take one metal and one leather. She'll put her scent on it. The volunteer in the ring will put their scent on all of the others. The judge will place one of the dumbbells with Dixie's scent in the middle of the pile, and then Chyna will need to find the *one* dumbbell that smells like Dixie."

"Wow."

We watched in silence as the volunteer, Lenora Houston, scented all of the dumbbells and then moved aside. Naomi Keller approached Dixie with a clipboard. Dixie placed the metal dumbbell on the clipboard. Naomi Keller took the dumbbell and dropped it in the middle of the pile. She started to step away but then reached down and touched Dixie's dumbbell.

The crowd gasped.

"What?" Red asked.

"She touched Dixie's dumbbell." I gazed from him to the ring and then looked around the crowd, which had started to rumble. "She's not supposed to do that."

Naomi Keller finished adjusting the dumbbells and then stood up and smiled. "Are you ready?"

"Ready," Dixie responded.

"Send your dog."

Dixie turned and pointed to the pile. "Find mine."

Chyna trotted to the pile and, in meticulous fashion, sniffed each article. She returned to the one in the center, picked it up, trotted back to Dixie, and sat in front of her.

Naomi grimaced. "Take it."

Dixie reached down and took the dumbbell from Chyna's mouth. "Finish."

Dixie gave a hand signal, and Chyna walked around her and sat glued to Dixie's left side.

"Exercise finished."

Several people in the crowd clapped, but they were quickly shushed.

"Perfect," I whispered. "She was freakin' perfect."

They did the same exercise again with a leather dumbbell.

"Why two?" Red asked.

"I think the textures hold scents differently, but you'll need to ask Dixie to be sure."

Again, Naomi Keller touched the one dumbbell with Dixie's scent, adding her scent on top of Dixie's. Nevertheless, Chyna sniffed the pile, found the one leather article with Dixie's scent, and brought it back quickly.

"Wow," Red whispered. "This is intense."

"There's just one more exercise to go, the moving stand and examination."

"What's that?"

"Dixie and Chyna will heel, and then she'll give Chyna a command to stay while she walks away from her. Chyna has to stand still while the judge examines her."

"Considering all of the examinations she's had in the show ring, I'd think this would be fairly easy."

"It's not easy, and I don't trust the judge not to try one last thing to trip them up." I said a silent prayer and focused my phone on the ring.

Naomi Keller looked stressed as she stared at Dixie and Chyna. "Are you ready?"

Dixie glanced down to make sure Chyna was in proper position. "Ready."

"Forward."

Dixie took approximately ten steps forward, with Chyna glued to her side.

"Stand your dog."

Dixie placed a hand in front of Chyna's face. "Stand," she commanded and kept walking. She continued to a chalk line the judge had drawn on the mat and turned and faced Chyna.

Naomi Keller approached Chyna and began to examine her. Even to my untrained eyes, the examination seemed unusually thorough. The judge pressed down on Chyna's back, looked at her teeth and ears. She then traversed the length of her spine and her tail. The crowd was extremely displeased, and cries echoed out, *That's not fair.* Through it all, Chyna stood still and endured the humiliation.

"My ob/gyn wasn't that invasive," B.J. whispered.

Dixie frowned, and it seemed as though steam came from her ears. Her chest heaved, and her eyes narrowed.

When the crowd noise grew to a low roar, Naomi ceased, but she took one step forward and somehow managed to step on Chyna's paw.

"Oh my God." I stared in disbelief. "She did that on purpose."

Through it all, Chyna was mute. Her shoulders drooped, but she did not move.

The crowd, however, was vocal and had begun to shout their disapproval.

Naomi Keller must have realized she'd gone too far. She took a step away. "Call your dog to heel."

"Chyna, heel."

Chyna limped to Dixie's side and sat in perfect heel position.

"Exercise finished." She walked to the table where the ring stewards sat, which was just a foot in front of where we were standing, and handed her scoresheet to the head steward.

The crowd erupted in applause and cheers.

Dixie bent down and checked her dog's paw and then marched up to Naomi Keller, reached back, and landed a right hook on the judge's chin.

Naomi Keller dropped to the ground like a rag doll.

After a brief moment of silent shock, the crowd cheered. Those who weren't standing before stood and applauded.

Dixie leaned down so her face was inches from Naomi Keller. "If you ever touch one of my dogs again, as God is my witness, I'll strangle you." Dixie turned back to Chyna and picked up her sixty-pound dog and carried her out of the ring.

Red turned to face me. "I had no idea dog shows were so exciting."

Chapter 4

We hurried out to Dixie's RV, where we found her sitting on the sofa hugging Chyna and crying.

"*You* were amazing," B.J. said. "Your competition was pretty darned good too, but you dropped that witch like George Foreman dropped Joe Frazier."

"Shush," Monica Jill said, giving B.J. a shove. "Is Chyna okay?"

Dixie sniffed. "I think so, but . . . I knew she didn't like me, and I expected her dirty tricks, like trying to cover my scent on the articles, but—"

"Speaking of that, how did you do it?" Madison asked. "I mean, she touched the dumbbell with your scent."

"I trained my dogs to look for the hot scent and ignore all others. Plus, Chyna has always been really reliable." She snuggled her face in Chyna's coat.

"I'd say she deserves a huge jackpot," I said.

"I almost forgot." Dixie hopped up and went to the treat jar. She pulled out a large pile of dried liver and placed it in front of Chyna.

All the other dogs immediately gave Dixie and the liver their full and complete attention, and she disbursed a small treat to each of them.

"So, what happens now?" I asked.

Dixie shook her head. "If she doesn't have me arrested for assault . . ." She glanced at Red.

He held his hands up. "I didn't see anything."

"It doesn't matter, there are plenty of videotapes. I'll probably be banned from competing for the rest of my life. I'll lose my ability to judge. In fact, I'll probably be banned from all dog shows for life." She took a deep breath and looked lovingly down at Chyna. "But it was worth it."

B.J. nudged Red. "Didn't I tell you it would be on like Donkey Kong?" She cracked her knuckles and bounced on her feet. "I think we should go and rough her up some more."

Monica Jill pinched B.J. "Would you stop that? We are *not* going to rough up anybody." She winked. "No matter how much we may want to."

Dixie smiled. "I appreciate all of you, but I am not encouraging violence." She gave us all a stern look. "What I did was wrong. I shouldn't have hit her, but . . ." She gave Chyna's head a rub. "Chyna was working so hard. She knew this was important to me, and she was so good, despite everything Naomi did to her. She just gave it her all and worked so well, and when I saw Naomi deliberately step on her foot—and Chyna didn't move, didn't bark or snap or anything—I just couldn't take it." Her eyes overflowed.

I hugged Dixie. "I understand completely." When we were done, Red handed me a handkerchief, and I wiped my eyes.

"Why don't we give Dixie some time?" Red said. He tugged on my sleeve and whispered, "I need to talk to you."

I turned to follow him out, but there was a knock on the door.

"Here it comes," Dixie said. She stood tall and braced herself. "Come in."

Lenora Houston climbed inside. She glanced around like a frightened cat. When her eyes landed on Red, she said, "You better come with me."

In a flash, something switched. Red was no longer my boyfriend hanging out with friends on a Saturday morning. Instead, he was Red Olson, TBI officer. I'm not sure what he did or how, but he was all law enforcement. "Stay here."

He followed Lenora Houston out of the RV.

We waited a half second and then followed him, leaving all of the dogs behind. Outside, we heard a loud commotion and followed the noise into the building.

Inside, there was a tight crowd and shouts. We pushed our way toward the front. Naomi Keller stood in the middle of the ring, drenched from head to toe with a sticky brown liquid.

"Is that . . . syrup?" Dixie asked.

B.J. sniffed. "Smells like it."

"Mercy," Monica Jill said.

Red grabbed a young woman wearing a Save the Greyhound T-shirt, who was holding a bucket that I guessed had once held the syrup. He dragged the woman out of the ring. The crowd parted to allow them to pass, whether from the sheer power of his authority or a desire to avoid getting the sticky syrup on them.

In the ring, Naomi Keller stood dripping with syrup, looking like a drenched rat.

"I kind of feel sorry for her now," I said. At least I did until Lenora Houston rushed into the ring and handed the bedraggled judge a towel, only to have it tossed back in her face.

"Your club will be paying for this." She waved her hands from her head to her feet. "You're going to pay for all of this. I've been humiliated, assaulted and now this . . . UGH." She stomped out of the ring.

A gray-haired man approached her. "Naomi, what on earth?"

"Don't start with me, Warren." Naomi shoved the man in the chest and left a sticky brown handprint on his previously pristine white shirt.

Dixie and Monica Jill stared at me. B.J. took it one step further and held up her hand like a wounded dog's paw and gave me a sad look, reminding me of what Naomi had done to poor Chyna.

"I said I *almost* feel sorry for her."

"Regardless of how you feel about the woman, you have to admit," Dr. Morgan said, "Naomi Keller is having a very bad day."

Outside, Red and a uniformed policeman were having an intense conversation with the man with the syrup handprint on his shirt, while the syrup-tosser sat in the back of a patrol car.

Try as I might, I couldn't catch any of the conversation, even though Mr. Syrup Print was extremely animated and waved his arms as though he were directing traffic at Hamilton Place Mall during Christmas.

"I wonder what that's all about."

When the arm waving slowed to the level needed to land a plane on an aircraft carrier, the policeman opened the back door, releasing his captive.

A wave of emotion washed over me as I remembered the one time when I had been arrested. That open door reminded me how grateful I'd been to experience freedom after the authorities thought I'd killed my husband.

Monica Jill patted my back. "You okay?"

"Fine."

B.J. gave me the *Whatchu talkin' 'bout, Willis* look. "Am I missing something?"

Once freed, Mr. Syrup Print attempted to place an arm around the syrup-tosser, but she wasn't having it. We watched as she pushed him away, ran to a Mini Cooper, and sped down the road, spitting gravel in her wake.

"What do you suppose that was all about?" I asked.

Dixie sighed. "I think that means family time at the Kellers' is going to be rough this year."

We stared at Dixie.

"Brittney is Warren's daughter and Naomi's stepdaughter."

Monica Jill, B.J., and I stood there, gawking at our friend.

"Wait a minute," Monica Jill said, leaning forward. "You mean to tell me that man is Warren? The one Naomi Keller just treated like dirt inside the building is her husband?"

Dixie nodded.

B.J. put a hand on her hip and glanced down her nose. "Are you saying that the woman who just staged a protest at a dog show aimed at nothing but public humiliation . . . that girl who just threw *syrup* on a woman wearing a suit in front of a crowd of people . . . that was Naomi's stepdaughter?"

Dixie nodded.

I shook my head like an Etch A Sketch to clear my brain, but still I had no words.

B.J. nudged Monica Jill. "This is going to be good. Let's go."

We headed toward the other massive RV parked at the club. Similar to Dixie, Naomi Keller had a luxury RV that looked large enough to house a third-world country. She had demanded access to water and electricity in her judging contract, so she was able to shower and remove the physical signs of her attack. Whether she was able to wash away the emotional signs was yet to be determined.

Red rejoined our group. He looked at me. "Hey, can we talk?"

I nodded and was about to follow him when a small red sports car sped through the parking lot. It barely missed B.J.'s SUV as it skidded to a stop.

"Hey, watch my car," B.J. yelled.

The driver wasn't listening and threw open the door and ran from her car toward Naomi Keller's RV.

"Not again," Red said. He passed Steve Austin's leash back to me and rushed after the woman.

"This can't be good," Dixie said and hurried after him.

"What now?" B.J. asked.

I took several steps and noticed that Dr. Morgan wasn't following. I turned to look back.

He shrugged. "I'll pass on this drama."

I handed him Steve Austin's leash and then hurried after my friends. I followed the shouts to the RV. Red was already inside, and Dixie, Monica Jill, and B.J. were just inside the door.

"GET OUT!" Naomi Keller screamed.

"HOMEWRECKER! You filthy little adulteress."

I heard Red trying to calm the two women. Based on the sound of their voices, I pitied him.

"You stay away from my husband, or I'll kill you. I'll kill you!"
Naomi Keller laughed.

There was a large crash as something breakable hit the wall.

"You'll pay for that!" Naomi screamed.

B.J., Monica Jill, and Dixie scrambled down the stairs and outside just as Red descended. He had a bear hug on the woman and was practically carrying her down the stairs. She kicked and wiggled, but Red didn't let go. Once he had her outside, he backed her against the RV.

"If you don't settle down, I'll be forced to handcuff you."

The woman looked at him—really looked at him for what was probably the first time.

He held up his shield and a pair of handcuffs for her to see he meant business.

She stared for a few moments and then, like a balloon that has been deflated, slid to the ground and wailed.

Red looked at me as though to say, *You have got to be joking.*

Dixie, Monica Jill, and I hurried to his aid. We helped the woman up and into Dixie's RV. The woman was sobbing so hard she could barely breathe. Dr. Morgan had been lounging with a lap full of German Shepherd, but once he caught sight of the hysterical woman, he helped us calm her down. When she finally stopped gasping for air and was able to breathe, we all relaxed.

Monica Jill made a cup of tea and passed it to her. Dixie got a blanket from a closet and wrapped it around the woman's shoulders. Even B.J. made herself useful and stood by, fanning the woman with a magazine she'd found.

"Just try and relax." Dixie plumped a pillow and stuck it behind the woman's back.

Dr. Morgan removed two of the dogs from the sofa to allow the woman to recline.

Once she was situated, we stood by, staring at her. After a few awkward moments, she looked as though she wanted to say something but suddenly stopped, her lip quivering, and we could tell the waterworks were about to start again.

Dixie surprised us by grabbing the woman by the shoulders and giving her a shake. "Now, June, I know you're upset, but you need to pull yourself together."

Whether due to the shock of Dixie's actions or not, the woman stared for several moments and then laughed. It started out as a chuckle but grew bigger. The laughter broke the tension, and everyone relaxed.

B.J. stopped fanning June and turned the magazine on herself. "Thank God. I thought I was going to have to slap you."

Monica Jill nudged her friend. "Will you stop scaring this poor woman." She leaned down and said, "Please, don't pay her any attention."

"June, these are my friends," Dixie said. "Monica Jill Nelson, Bobbie Jean Thompson."

"Call me B.J."

"Dr. Morgan." Dixie pointed to the doctor, who gave a slight bow.

I smiled when Dixie pointed to me. "Lilly Ann Echosby."

She turned to Red. "And this is Lilly Ann's friend, Dennis Olson."

Red stepped forward and held out a hand. "Please, call me Red."

The smile she had on her face when introduced to the rest of us froze when she shook Red's hand. However, Dixie smiled and chatted as though her friend hadn't just had a minor breakdown. "Everyone, I'd like you to meet June Vannover."

We all said hello.

Dr. Morgan stood. "I signed up for two trials, and I think it's about time Max and I headed out for round two."

If it were a real competition, we would only be able to enter once per day. However, since it was a mock trial and didn't really count, Dixie encouraged us to sign up multiple times. However, I'd already missed my second trial, so I stayed.

"Snoball and I have another trial too," B.J. said. She scooped up her little white highland terrier and reluctantly made her way toward the door. "Monica Jill, are you coming?"

"Jac and I have had our fill of public humiliation for one day, but I'll come and cheer on my friends."

B.J., Monica Jill, and Dr. Morgan left, taking their dogs with them, which left the RV a lot quieter.

Dixie patted June Vannover on the leg. "Now, you drink your tea and tell us what's wrong."

I couldn't help but be impressed by the way Dixie managed to not only put June at ease but set her up to spill her guts.

June sipped slowly, but she eventually realized she would need to talk sooner or later. She gulped her tea and looked up. "I'm sorry for making a scene. It's just . . . well, I've known Naomi Keller for years . . . I thought she was my friend." She swallowed hard to hold back the emotion. "She and Dixon . . . they're . . . she said she's pregnant. We tried for years, but I just couldn't . . . Dixon said it was my fault. I went to so many doctors, and they said there was nothing wrong with me, but Dixon said it was my fault. He wanted children, and I couldn't . . . when he found out that she was carrying his child, he said it proved he had been right, and I was the problem." She swallowed hard. "He told me he wanted a divorce." The tears flowed down her cheeks. "He's leaving me because I can't give him children and she can. He's leaving me for that . . . that . . ."

"Why, the dirty little homewrecker," Dixie said.

Something in June Vannover's eyes took me back to a year ago when I had learned my husband, Albert, was having an affair. I saw the same look of incredible disbelief in her that I'd worn for months when Albert dropped that bomb on me. Something in me immediately connected to June Vannover, and without thinking, I reached out and pulled her into a hug. Initially, she must have been as shocked by my action as I was. I held her stiff body and whispered. "I've been in your shoes." Something in those words loosened the floodgates. She relaxed and gripped me with both arms and sobbed. We both sat there on the sofa in Dixie's RV and sobbed until neither one of us had any tears left to cry. When we finished and broke apart, we looked at each other and laughed.

Dixie, who had also sobbed, stood up and passed us a box of tissues. "We all look like a hot mess."

I looked from Dixie to June Vannover and saw eyeliner- and mascara-ringed eyes that were red and puffy from crying. Their previously perfect foundation was now tear-streaked.

I glanced around at Red, who was quietly standing near the door, looking as though he'd rather be anywhere else than trapped in an RV with three crying women. His expression made me laugh even more. Realizing that some of his anxiety was due to the fact that he was concerned for me made me want to give him a break. "I think we can handle it from here, if you want to—"

"Yes. I'll be outside." He rushed out the door.

Dixie, June, and I glanced at each other and laughed again.

"That poor man," Dixie said.

June pointed. "He's not the . . ."

I scowled and shook my head. "Good God, NO! That's Red . . . my boyfriend." I suppressed a desire to giggle like a schoolgirl. I quickly shared my story of how my husband, Albert, had dumped me after twenty-five years of marriage.

"Weren't you upset? How did you . . . how could you move on? I feel so betrayed, but . . I don't want a divorce. I know it's all *that* woman!" She huffed and pointed in the general direction of Naomi Keller's RV. "She bewitched him. She told him lies, and she's just using him. She doesn't care about Dixon. I know she doesn't. She doesn't have a heart."

"Initially, I felt the same way. I didn't want a divorce . . . at first. I was comfortable. We'd been together for so long, I didn't know anything else. I didn't know what it was like to be on my own."

June stared at me as though I'd just unlocked the secrets to life. "How did you do it?"

I smiled. "One night, I met a woman on a train named Miss Florrie. She was a wise older woman. She looked at me and said, 'Honey, whatever he did, it ain't worth all them tears.'"

"How did she know it was a man?"

"I asked the same thing. She said, 'Only a man can make a woman cry like you was crying. And baby, ain't *no* man worth crying over. Tears are a precious commodity. You shouldn't waste them on someone that done you wrong.'"

June gazed at me with wide eyes. "Was she a psychic?"

I thought for a moment. "Honestly, I think she was just a wise woman who had lived through a lot and understood . . . people." I shared how Miss Florrie helped me realize that Albert and I hadn't been happy for quite some time and that life was too short not to be happy. "She's the one who led me to Chattanooga."

"How?"

"She told me I needed to find my *happy place*." I shrugged. "I realized I didn't want to live in Indiana anymore. I wanted to be someplace warm. I wanted to be around my friend." I reached out and squeezed Dixie's hand. "And . . . I wanted a dog."

June leaned forward. "So, you just left? You moved to Chattanooga?" I nodded.

"What did your husband say? Didn't he try to stop you?"

"Actually, he was killed, so he didn't really say anything, but it wouldn't have mattered." I gazed at her. "I'm not saying that's what you should do."

"You can find your happy place," Dixie said and smiled.

"But what will I do? What if being with Dixon is what makes me happy?"

"No one can answer that question for you," I said. "You have to decide what makes you happy, but you can't force someone to stay with you if that's not what they want."

She nodded, but I wasn't sure she fully believed me.

We talked a bit longer, but eventually June Vannover said she was going to go home and talk to her husband and decide what she should do.

I wasn't sure she was ready to find her happy place, but I didn't know what else I could say or do. Eventually, I decided to leave it up to Providence and went in search of Red.

I didn't have to go far to find him. When I did, I gave him a hug. "Thank you."

"What did I do?"

"For being here. For being supportive. For helping me feel loved."

"My pleasure." He held me tight and kissed me thoroughly. "Actually, I have an important question I've been trying to ask."

"What question?"

He opened his mouth to answer, but a bloodcurdling scream echoed through the building. We glanced around to find the source of the disruption.

Monica Jill stumbled inside. She took two steps toward us. "She's dead." Then she stopped and crumbled to the floor in a dead faint.

"Not again," Red mumbled as he pushed his way through the crowd.

Chapter 5

Monica Jill opened her eyes. "What happened?"

"Thank God," B.J. said and flopped into a chair, fanning herself.

"You fainted," Dixie said. She placed a wet compress on Monica Jill's head. "We had to get two guys to carry you back here."

Monica Jill, resting on the sofa in Dixie's RV, said, "I've never fainted a day in my life."

"Well, you certainly fainted today," B.J. said.

Monica Jill shook her head. "Nope. I don't faint."

"Pig-headed," B.J. mumbled.

Dixie gave B.J. a frown and then turned back to Monica Jill. "She's right. You absolutely fainted this time. Dr. Morgan looked at you. He's going to take care of . . ." She looked around, unsure whether she should share the bad news now or wait. She glanced in my direction.

I shrugged.

"Dr. Morgan promised he'd come back and give you a thorough checkup as soon as he can."

"Oh, no, he won't." Monica Jill sat up too quickly and swayed a bit before lying back down. "I'm absolutely fine. I certainly don't need to be checked out by a coroner." She closed her eyes. After a few moments, she said, "I probably just need to eat something. I'm just going to lie here for a few moments until the room stops swaying, and then I'm going to go home."

We exchanged glances.

B.J. leaned forward. "You listen here, you skinny little pageant queen. You are going to lie there and get examined by Dr. Morgan as soon as he gets back, and if you think we're going to let you get behind the wheel of a car, then you have another think coming."

Monica Jill opened her eyes and stared at B.J. She must have noticed the steely stare she received and figured out that B.J. meant business. She sighed and felt her hair. "Why am I soaking wet?"

Dixie and I stared at B.J.

"We had to revive you." B.J. turned to Dixie. "I'm going to need something stronger than coffee."

Dixie got a bottle of wine from one of the upper cabinets and poured three glasses and passed them around.

"Where's mine?" Monica Jill said.

"You can't even sit up." B.J. took a sip. "You just lie back down there and wait until Dr. Morgan gets back, or I'll tie you to that sofa."

For a half second, Monica Jill looked as though she wanted to challenge B.J.'s authority, but a narrow-eyed glance from B.J. made her realize she didn't stand a chance. She sighed and lay back on her pillow. "I can't just lie here in wet clothes."

B.J. reached over and tossed a towel to her friend. "Stop whining, and be thankful I couldn't get the defibrillator off the wall."

A look of pure fear crossed Monica Jill's face, but she closed her mouth and dried her arms, face, and hair to the best of her ability while still lying flat on her back. When she was done, she folded the towel and glanced at us. "Is someone going to tell me what happened?"

We exchanged glances, and Dixie sat next to Monica Jill on the sofa. "Do you remember anything?"

Monica Jill squinted and frowned. "The last thing I remember is watching a beautiful cocker spaniel compete. It was dark brown and just a beautiful dog." She looked at Dixie. "You know, we used to have cocker spaniels when I was growing up." She thought a moment and then shook her head. "I don't really remember much after the cocker spaniel."

Dixie patted her hand. "Don't worry about trying to remember. I'm sure it will come back to you." She hesitated. "Naomi Keller is dead."

"Dead?" Monica Jill propped herself up on one elbow and glanced at the group. "How did she die? What happened?"

"We were hoping you could tell us," Dixie said quietly.

"Me?"

"You found her."

Monica Jill flopped back on her pillow. "I don't remember anything. I remember the cocker spaniel, and then I woke up here." She glanced at B.J. "Soaking wet."

B.J. sipped her wine and ignored the dig.

"Don't worry yourself."

We sat in silence for a few minutes and then talked about everything except the elephant in the room, Naomi Keller's murder. After a strained, prolonged silence, Dr. Morgan joined us.

He looked at Monica Jill's eyes and examined her head for bumps, while we all watched anxiously. "She's had a bit of a shock, but she'll be fine."

Monica Jill swung her legs off the sofa and sat up. "Great. Thank you. Now, would you tell these prison guards I'm perfectly fine to drive myself home." She stuck out her tongue at B.J.

"Hold on. I didn't say anything about you driving."

"Ha!" B.J. stuck out her tongue.

Monica Jill looked crestfallen. "What? You can't be serious. You said I was okay."

"I did say that, but you've also had a shock. You've fainted, and you're suffering from short-term memory loss. I think you should allow one of us to drive you home, or I can call your husband to come get you. Take it easy over the weekend and make an appointment to see your regular doctor first thing Monday morning."

"But . . . I don't need to see a doctor. I feel fine." She pouted.

"Do you want some cheese?" B.J. asked.

Monica Jill frowned. "Cheese?"

"I just thought you might want cheese to go along with all that whining."

Monica Jill scowled at her friend and then looked around to find her purse. "Oh, stop gloating and take me home." She glared. "How many glasses of wine have you had?"

"Not nearly enough," B.J. said.

"Where's Jac?"

"When you fainted, he started howling," Dixie said. "We put him in a crate in the office so he wouldn't disturb you." She went to get him.

B.J. stood up. "I better get Snoball."

When all of the women left, I turned to Dr. Morgan. "I haven't talked to Red since all of this happened, but do you know how she died?"

"It's just a guess at the moment. We won't know for sure until the autopsy, but I'd say she was strangled." He paused. "With a dog leash."

Chapter 6

B.J. drove Monica Jill home, and I went in search of Red. I ran into Madison Cooper inside taking names and addresses from the dog show participants. When she caught my eye, she finished up and came over and gave me a hug.

"We have got to stop meeting like this," she said.

I glanced around. "Where's Red?"

She tilted her head in the direction of Naomi Keller's RV. "He's still working with the local police."

I leaned close. "Any idea who did it?"

She shook her head. "If he knows, he hasn't shared it with me. I'm just a peon stuck doing the grunt work." She held up her notepad. "I don't mind. I know I'm new and was only hired for my skills as a computer hacker, but . . . I probably know more about dogs than any of them."

"You think her death had something to do with dogs?"

"I'm not sure, really, but that lead she was strangled with, it—" She stopped short, fearing she'd revealed a deep secret.

I waved away her fears. "I already knew she was strangled with a leash. In fact, the way information spreads in the dog community, I'd say almost everyone here probably knows by now."

She breathed a sigh of relief. "It's just that—"

"Are you Madison?" A uniformed policeman interrupted our discussion. She nodded.

Steve Austin tugged at the end of a leash. "That TBI officer wanted to know if you could take his dog to someone named . . . Lilly?"

I reached out my hand to take the leash. "I'm Lilly." Steve Austin had already recognized me. He stood on his back legs and had both paws on my shoulders. He was licking my face and doing his best to hoist his eighty pounds into my arms.

The policeman passed over the leash and made a quick exit.

Steve Austin was in dire need of attention and was in no mood to wait. I struggled to get the large dog off.

Thankfully, Dixie came over. "OFF." She took the leash and gave a correction and then gazed into the dog's eyes.

To my surprise, Steve Austin sat and returned Dixie's gaze. Butt and all four paws on the ground, he didn't move. After a few moments, Dixie smiled. "Good boy." She reached into a pocket and gave the dog a huge jackpot of dried liver.

Red walked up. "I don't know how you managed it, but I need to know your secret."

Dixie petted the dog. "He's a good boy. He just needs more training."

"No, seriously. How did you do that? Did you hypnotize him?"

Dixie gave him a long stare. "When you're on the job, there's something about you that changes. Lilly says you flip the switch and go into law-enforcement mode."

He shrugged. "I guess, but I don't even realize I'm doing it, but . . . okay."

"I've watched, and you become very . . . authoritative."

He chuckled. "You mean bossy."

"Not exactly, it's just you know you have a job to do, and you do it." She glanced down at the pit bull/Labrador mix. "Dogs are pack animals and need a leader, an alpha. It's the leader's responsibility to look after the pack and keep them safe. As the owner, that's your job." She narrowed her gaze. "Keep in mind, I'm not saying you become harsh or abusive, but you need to be authoritative. Dogs recognize that authority and respond."

We gazed down at Steve Austin, who was scouring the floor for crumbs.

"If you worked with him, I think he has the potential to be as good as Turbo and maybe could be useful in policework."

Red's eyes widened. "Turbo is a trained police dog." He gazed down at Steve Austin, who had devoured every crumb but was sitting calmly gazing at Dixie, waiting for another treat.

"Turbo wasn't born trained to do search and rescue and Schutzhund. Joe worked hard to train him. If you worked with Steve Austin, he has the drive and the personality to do it too."

"Remind me again, what's Schutzhund?" Red asked.

Dixie went into teaching mode. "Schutzhund is a German word meaning 'protection dog.' It's been around since around the early 1900s. Police and military use it, but it's also a dog sport. It focuses on tracking, obedience, and protection."

We all gazed at the dog.

Red let me know that he had several more hours of work. "Just because I have to stay doesn't mean you do."

"I think I'll take Aggie home. Would you like me to take Steve Austin?"

His eyes lit up. "Yes, please. I'll stop by to get him as soon as I can get away."

I packed up the dogs and drove home. I was thankful for a large, fenced-in backyard. I let Aggie and Steve Austin out and allowed them to run and play before I let out Rex, my tiny Toy Poodle puppy.

Rex was a small, silver poodle I'd adopted a few months ago when his owner was murdered. Aggie and Rex were small, especially when compared with the other dogs in our circle of friends. Between Dixie's two Standard Poodles, Dr. Morgan's German Shepherd, Monica Jill's mixed breed, Jac, and my daughter Stephanie's Golden Retriever and her boyfriend Joe's Plott Hound, Turbo, there were a lot of large dogs. Initially, I was concerned about the small puppy getting injured. However, I was amazed by the tenderness I saw demonstrated whenever the dogs were all together. Occasionally, one of the big dogs would be unable to make a sudden stop when running and would roll one of the smaller dogs, but I was astonished that the larger dogs often worked hard to avoid deliberately colliding with the smaller dogs. After watching the dogs burn up energy running and playing, I felt confident that Rex would be fine.

My phone rang, and I smiled when I saw my son David's picture appear on the screen. "Hey, how is everything in the Big Apple?"

David was an actor who had just returned from a successful tour in Italy and was, I thought, preparing to head to Australia and New Zealand.

"Hi, Mom. Things in general are great in New York."

My mom radar went up with the distinction. "Okay . . . how are things, specifically?"

"I'm fine, but I can't say as much for the plumbing in my apartment."

I heaved a sigh of relief. "What's happened to the plumbing? I thought you were remodeling?"

"I am, but . . . a pipe broke, and my apartment flooded, and, well, it's a real mess."

"I'm so sorry, dear. How bad was the flood damage?"

He spent the next five minutes sharing. It sounded horrible, and practically everything he owned was ruined. The flood happened overnight, while he was away, and wasn't discovered until the water leaked down and was coming through the ceiling of his downstairs neighbor. So, he now had mold damage to contend with. "The insurance will cover the damage, but . . . the drywall will need to be replaced."

"Oh, honey. That's awful. What can I do to help?"

"I was hoping you'd ask." I could hear the smile in his voice. "Any chance I could rent your spare room for a couple of weeks?"

"Of course, you're always welcome, and you know it. I'd love for you to come." Now I was smiling. "I'm sure Madison will be happy to see you too."

"I'll be excited to see her as well, although she may not have much time for me now that she's a TBI hacker and working crime scenes. Which reminds me, what the heck is happening? Did I understand that someone was murdered at your dog show?"

Thanks to the speed of twenty-first-century technology, David had already heard about Naomi Keller's murder. I filled him in on the few bits and pieces of information I knew, which really wasn't much. However, I couldn't shake the feeling that there was something I knew but had forgotten. No matter how I tried, I couldn't remember what it was, but experience taught me that if I stopped trying to force myself to remember, it would resurface.

David had apparently been confident that he would be welcome and had booked a flight into Chattanooga for tomorrow. I wrote down his flight information and promised I'd be there to pick him up. We chatted a bit longer, but then I got another call.

"It must be my lucky day. Stephanie's calling."

David and I ended our call, and I switched over to talk to my daughter.

"I just got off the phone with your brother. Is it my birthday? Mother's Day? Or am I just one lucky woman?"

Stephanie chuckled. "I hope you didn't get off the phone with David because of me."

I reassured her that we had finished our conversation and that I was looking forward to seeing him the next day, so it was no problem.

"Oh, I didn't realize David was coming down to Chattanooga," she said slowly.

"Why would that be a problem?"

"No problem. I have to go to Nashville for a conference, and I was thinking maybe I could mix business with pleasure and—"

"*Yes!* I have two spare bedrooms, and I'd love to have both of my children here for a visit."

She laughed. "Are you sure? I'd need to bring Lucky and—"

"You know I love Lucky. I can even keep him while you're at your conference, so you won't have to leave him in your hotel room while you're there."

"I was going to ask if you'd mind."

"Of course not. I love Lucky, and I know Aggie and Rex will be excited to see him too."

We chatted for a few more minutes, and I got the dates of her conference and the days that she'd be in town.

When I hung up, I couldn't help but smile at the thought of having both my children here to visit at the same time. Then I got down to practical measures and took inventory to make sure that everything was ready. This house wasn't large, but there was plenty of room for three adults and three dogs. Lucky was bigger than Aggie and Rex, and wouldn't fit in their crates, but he was so well behaved, he wouldn't need to be crated during the day. However, I would pick up a new Golden Retriever–sized dog bed the next time I went to the pet store.

When Red arrived later, he found me cleaning and making sure there were fresh linens available.

"Expecting company?" He glanced around the guest room.

Whenever a guest left, I immediately cleaned the room, put fresh linens on the beds, and made sure it was ready for my next guest. I then closed the door so the dogs wouldn't mess up my clean guest rooms. So, the fact that the guest-room doors were both open was likely the first giveaway that company was expected.

I smiled. "David and Stephanie are coming at the same time. I'm super excited." I dusted the nightstands and headboards and made sure the room was perfect.

He yawned and stretched. "I can tell."

"I'm sorry. You must be exhausted. Are you hungry?"

He sniffed. "I wasn't until I smelled whatever you've got cooking in that crockpot in the kitchen."

"I put a roast in this morning. I planned to make French dip sandwiches." I glanced at my watch. "They should be ready soon. I was going to make some potato salad to go with them, but . . ." I looked down at the vacuum cleaner and duster. "I got distracted."

"I can make the potato salad. You finish what you're doing."

My former military TBI officer loved to cook. He said it helped eliminate stress. Whatever it did for him, I was more than happy to enjoy the benefits. Although my clothes were getting a little snug since I'd started dating him. As a member of law enforcement, he had a rigid schedule that required a certain level of physical fitness. As an accountant, I didn't have the same requirements. However, running after Aggie and Rex was definitely increasing my activity level. Plus, once they had the basics of obedience down, I planned to start training for canine agility. From what I'd seen on television, it looked like running around an obstacle course was going to provide a lot of exercise for all of us.

I finished dusting the rooms and made sure both guest rooms were ready. By the time I was satisfied with the results, I heard Red removing plates from the cabinet and knew dinner was ready. When I went into the kitchen, he had just plated our meals.

"Perfect timing," he said and handed me a plate with a beautifully toasted bun with cheese and mushrooms and a small ramekin with a delicious au jus.

It was still sunny, so we decided to eat outside on the back deck, which allowed the dogs to play while we enjoyed our meals.

My single-story house was in a neighborhood that my realtor, Monica Jill, called transitional, but I'd call it eclectic. Before choosing my house, I viewed one of the other homes that was for sale in this neighborhood. If I had to hazard a guess, I'd say the houses were probably considered luxurious back in the 1980s when they were built. Unfortunately, neither of them had been updated for the twenty-first century and were woefully outdated. On the plus side, they both had great bones. The house next door had the most hideous carpeting I'd ever seen, but I'm sure it had been all the rage when it was purchased, along with the atrium windows and outdoor carpeting that covered the patio. I'd chosen the house with great windows and light that had undergone a sprucing up sometime in the past forty years and, while still in need of updates, was livable.

"Penny for your thoughts."

"You would be wasting your money." I shook my head to clear it of house renovations. "I'm sorry, dear. I was thinking about the house and wondering if I will ever be able to afford to renovate it the way I want to. Or even if I should."

"Why not?" He reached across and squeezed my hand. "Not having buyer's remorse already, are you? When do you close?"

"Six more days."

When I'd found this house, I had every intention of buying it, but when my bank ran my credit, they discovered that, despite the fact that he was dead, my late husband was purchasing houses and cars and taking out loans that had damaged any credit he might need in the afterlife, and it had caused harm to my own ability to purchase. Thankfully, the seller was willing to let me rent the house while my daughter, Stephanie, put all of her talent as a lawyer to work and not only located the identity thief but had him prosecuted.

"I'm excited to have a house of my own, but I don't know if I'll price myself out of the resale market if I put too much money into the renovations."

"I'm pretty handy, and I'd be willing to help with the renovations to help keep the cost down."

"Thank you, but you're a busy man, and I don't want to test your patience or the strength of our relationship with a major renovation project." I laughed. "Not yet, anyway."

"Speaking of testing our relationship." He cleared his throat. "I've been trying to ask you something all day. I suppose now is as good a time as any."

"Okaaay . . . fire away."

He took a deep breath. "I was wondering . . . we've been dating for several months now, and you know that I care about you very deeply . . ."

"I care about you too."

He inhaled deeply. "I wanted to ask you . . . I mean . . ."

"Red, just ask me whatever it is you want to ask."

He nodded, took a deep breath, and blurted out, "Would you be willing to meet my family?"

"I'd love to meet your family." I leaned across the table and kissed him. "See, that wasn't so hard."

"All of them?"

I stopped with my sandwich midway to my mouth. "When you say all . . . you mean . . ."

He nodded. "My mom and all of my sisters and their husbands and kids and, well, all of them."

"All five of your sisters?"

"I've pushed my mom off as long as I can, and now she's gotten my sisters involved. Last night, they held an intervention."

"An intervention? To meet me?"

He nodded. "They ganged up on me. My mom started talking about how she didn't have much time left and how before she went to meet her maker, she wanted to see her baby was going to be taken care of." He colored. "I mean, you would have thought she had one foot in the grave and that I was still in diapers."

I tried to hold it in but couldn't and burst out laughing. Eventually, Red joined me. When we finally stopped, I leaned back in my chair. "Since I'm going to be closing on the house and David and Stephanie are coming, what if I invited your family here. Monica Jill suggested we have a housewarming party, but what if we had a barbecue?"

He glanced around at the yard. "I think that would be great. This yard is amazing, and it could definitely hold a lot of people." He gave me a very serious look. "Are you sure?"

"Of course, I'm sure. I can invite my friends from the dog club and maybe even a few folks from the museum."

We spent the next hour talking through the plans for a housewarming party. Red wrote down the to-do items, while I wrote down the details of the party plans. By the time he left, we had several pages of notes on things we needed to complete. Despite the butterflies in my stomach about the thought of meeting Red's family, I was excited. I'd had a few other gatherings since moving to Chattanooga, but this would be the official This-House-Belongs-To-Me party. We set a date for the next Saturday.

When Red and Steve Austin left, I walked around the house and took inventory. The bedrooms would, of course, be off-limits. The living room, dining room, and kitchen would need a few small touches, but nothing major. If the weather was good, most people would spend their time in the backyard.

Red was right. The backyard was the property's main attraction. One of the main reasons I'd bought the house was because of the private yard, with its huge, multi-tiered deck, which the previous owner had built around the tall mature trees that dotted the property. I was sure I could rent some extra tables and chairs, and there would be plenty of room for even Red's large family.

I sent text messages to Dixie, Monica Jill, and Stephanie, and they were all eager to help with the preparations. Red must have called his mother from the car because he sent a text message saying that his mother had accepted the invitation before he had time to get home. I forced myself not to get nervous. It was just a housewarming. I'd be surrounded by friends and family and people who cared about me. We'd have food and drinks and a good time. I lay in bed and tossed and turned and tried to relax. I glanced over at Aggie. "What could possibly go wrong?"

Chapter 7

On Sunday morning, I got up and went to an early church service. Even on days when I wasn't scrambling to cram five million things into a twenty-four-hour period, I preferred the early services. They weren't nearly as crowded as the mid-morning ones. I also found that I got a lot more accomplished when the service was over. When I was young, my grandmother used to say going to the earliest service was putting God first, and if I did that, He would help me with the rest of my day. As I've gotten older, I suspect that it's because the eleven a.m. service cuts into the day. Regardless of the reason, it worked. By noon, I had gone to church, visited the grocery store, eaten breakfast, and gotten dinner started in my slow cooker before I headed out to the airport to pick up David.

My youngest, David, was in his early twenties, slender, with curly dark hair. He walked out of the airport, and I quickly pulled over to the curb and popped the back hatch of my SUV, waving frantically to get his attention.

He spotted me and hurried over, tossed in his backpack, and pressed the button that lowered the door. He gave me a hug. "Mom, it's great to see you. Thanks for letting me crash."

I stood slightly confused. "I know with all of your traveling you've learned to pack light, but surely you have more luggage than that?"

He shook his head. "Most of my clothes were ruined by the flood."

Airport security circled, and we hurried to get in the car.

I pulled away from the curb. "You're taking the loss of your clothes pretty well."

He shrugged. "Thankfully, it's covered by insurance. Madison's going to help me replenish my wardrobe, so . . . I'm going to look at it as a 'shoppertunity.'"

David proclaimed himself to be on the verge of starvation, so I stopped at a local restaurant before going home.

Once settled at the restaurant, we placed our orders, and I got updated on his performances and upcoming plans. For most of his life, David had longed for a career on the stage. Despite the pressure applied by my late husband to convince him to go into a "reasonable" career, he followed his heart and pursued his dream. Against the odds, he'd found success and was doing extremely well. As I listened to him talk about commercials, small parts on television programs, and his current successful show, I was filled with pride and a bit of sadness. I was, of course, thankful that he was doing well. However, I also knew that David's success meant he would never be content to live anywhere outside of a bustling metropolis like New York or Los Angeles.

Our food arrived, and we made short work of it. David asked about the open house. He liked Red, but he knew I was nervous about meeting his large family. I was grateful he and Stephanie would both be there for moral support.

"What's this I hear about a murder at your dog club?"

I quickly told him about Naomi Keller's murder.

"So, are you going to get out your deerstalker and tackle another mystery?"

I shook my head. "Absolutely not."

"Why not? You've solved several murders, and I'm sure Red would appreciate the help."

"I'm sure Red would prefer if I didn't get involved and left sleuthing to the *professionals*."

He chuckled. "That never stopped you before."

I thought about that. "This is different. I didn't know Naomi Keller, and I didn't like what little I did know. Besides, I have my hands full with preparing to close on my house, planning a housewarming party, getting ready to compete in my first obedience trial, and meeting my boyfriend's family."

David sipped his sweet tea and smiled.

"What?"

"Nothing. All of that is true, but . . ."

"But what?"

"But I know my mom, and I don't think you will be able to leave a mystery unsolved."

"Under normal circumstances, I'd agree with you."

"What's so abnormal about these circumstances? Apart from Dad, you didn't know most of the other people who were murdered."

"No, but in those cases, the police were concentrated on either me or someone I care about." I shook myself to ward off the heaviness that had descended over me like a cloak. "This time's different. All of my friends are above suspicion." I glanced up at David, and my motherly instincts kicked in. "Wait, what have you heard?"

David did a masterful job of avoiding eye contact, but I waited. If nothing else, I knew my son wouldn't be able to allow the silence to lag. Eventually, he began cracking his knuckles and tapping his fingers on the table, a sure sign he was nervous. "Nothing."

I stared at him and allowed the silence to drag on.

When the silence was too much, he caved. He leaned forward and whispered as though he were about to pass along confidential government secrets. "Okay, but I was sworn to secrecy, and if Madison knows I told, then . . . she won't trust me."

I reached across and patted his hand. "I'm your mother. Anything you tell me is safe."

He took a deep breath. "I don't think Red is included in this, but she said Aunt Dixie was one of the top suspects."

"Dixie? You have got to be kidding me. Dixie would never hurt anyone."

He flapped his hands to shush me and looked around. I assumed he was checking to see if any TBI officers just happened to be sitting nearby and were monitoring our conversation.

"Dixie is the kindest, nicest, most peace-loving person," I said. "Okay, so she might have decked Naomi Keller, but that woman totally deserved it. She actually hurt Chyna." I huffed and tried to collect my thoughts. "And she might have *threatened* to strangle her . . ." I put my head in my hands. "Oh, God."

"In front of witnesses," David added.

"In front of a lot of witnesses, but . . . well, she was angry, and Naomi Keller was a horrid woman." I leaned forward. "You know she disqualified Dixie's entire class simply because she was angry at her . . . oh my." This was just getting worse and worse.

David nodded. "Because they had a history."

I tried to think, but my thoughts were racing in every direction. "But, surely, Red couldn't possibly—"

He shook his head. "Red absolutely does *not* believe Aunt Dixie murdered her, but . . . well . . ."

I read his thoughts, which were written all over his face. "But they think Red is biased because of me."

He nodded slowly.

"But Naomi Keller was a terrible person. There were tons of people who probably wanted to kill her." I ticked the names off one by one. "Her stepdaughter staged a protest and threw syrup on her. She was having an affair with June Vannover's husband, and June had threatened her. Plus, her husband was there and, well, if he didn't know his wife was having an affair before, he absolutely knew about it after June finished."

"I know, and Madison said Red mentioned all of that to his bosses at the TBI, but . . . they were concerned about his objectivity because . . ."

"Because of me."

"I'm sorry."

I stared at my son and realized none of this was his fault. In fact, if he hadn't told me, I doubt that Red would have. "Honey, I really do appreciate you telling me. I know it had to be hard for you." I patted his hand. "At least now I know what I have to do."

"What?"

"Whether I liked her or not, I have to figure out who murdered Naomi Keller."

Chapter 8

David and I finished lunch and headed home. Dixie's Lexus was in the driveway when we arrived. I had arranged for Dixie, Monica Jill, and B.J. to come by later in the afternoon for dinner and to help plan the housewarming. I glanced at my watch, even though I knew it was too early for dinner. One look at Dixie's face told me she was upset.

"What happened?" I stared at my friend, who was normally well coifed, with meticulous makeup. Her hair was pulled back into a messy ponytail, and she wasn't wearing makeup.

"I totally forgot that David was coming today." She hugged him. "I was so upset, I just got in the car and drove."

"It's okay, but let's go inside." I glanced around, but thankfully none of the neighbors were watching.

David took his backpack into the guest room he'd used during his last visit. After giving instructions for him to let Aggie and Rex out, Dixie and I went to the back deck. I grabbed a bottle of wine and three glasses on my way.

Outside, I poured the wine and waited.

Dixie sipped hers and took several deep breaths.

David opened the back door, and Aggie rushed out and greeted Dixie and me before running down, squatting, and taking care of business. Like a small shadow, Rex followed her from person to person and then went down to the grass and hiked his leg near a tree before rushing back up to the deck.

David scooped him up and gave him a scratch. He glanced over at Dixie. "I can go back inside if you two want privacy."

Dixie waved away his protests. She took another sip of wine. "It's perfectly fine. You'll find out soon enough."

David and I exchanged concerned looks but waited for Dixie to collect herself enough to talk.

Eventually, she took a deep breath and said, "I think they're going to arrest me for murdering Naomi Keller."

I glanced at David out of the corner of my eye before turning to my friend. "What makes you think that?"

She narrowed her eyes. "Wait. Neither of you seem surprised by this. Did Red tell you that he suspected me?"

"Red hasn't said anything to me," I hurriedly reassured her. "In fact, I'm sure he doesn't suspect you. He knows you. He knows you couldn't have killed anyone." I turned to David and silently asked for permission to share his secret.

He sighed and then quickly shared what he'd learned from Madison.

"I should have trusted Red." She leaned across and patted my hand. "I'm sorry."

"It's okay, but what makes you think you'd be arrested? Surely, Red didn't say—"

"No, it wasn't Red. It was some pencil-necked troll named Officer Martin. He came by the house at the break of dawn and asked a ton of questions. He insinuated that I killed Naomi Keller. I was so angry, I told him to get out and come back when he was ready to arrest me. He told me not to leave town. Can you believe that? In my own house . . . It was just too much. Beau's out of town on business, and it took everything in me not to call him to come home this instant."

"Oh, Dixie. I'm so sorry."

"It's not your fault. And I know it isn't Red's fault either. I'm just so angry and . . . well, embarrassed."

"What do you have to be embarrassed about?"

"I behaved so badly yesterday. I argued with her. I threatened her, and I actually struck her." She shook her head. "It's no wonder they think I killed her."

"Well, you weren't the only person who threatened her or the only person who attacked her. My goodness, in the short time that Naomi Keller was at the dog club, she managed to tick off a lot of people."

David got up and went inside. When he came back, he placed a notepad and pen on the table. "Okay, we better get this investigation underway." He grinned. "Who else had a reason to kill Naomi Keller?"

I looked at Dixie. "You knew her better than me."

She thought for a moment. "Well, there's her stepdaughter, Brittney."

"Why did she hate her stepmother so much?"

"The gossip around town is that Brittney never forgave Naomi for ruining her parents' marriage."

"Wait, so Naomi had an affair with—"

"Warren Keller."

"So Dixon Vannover isn't the first married man she's gone after?"

Dixie shook her head. "Sadly, no. The joke around town is that Naomi Keller built her husband's fortune by ruining marriages." David and I must have looked confused because she added, "Warren is a divorce attorney."

"Wow."

David tapped his pen. "Who is that guy you mentioned . . . Dixon Vannover?"

Dixie poured more wine into her glass and leaned back in her chair. "A local politician with aspirations of being in the White House."

I stared at Dixie as recognition finally hit me. "He's on the board of the museum. And I've seen his political ads on television. He's young, super tanned, with perfect hair and dazzling white teeth." I thought for a moment. "Isn't he the one that wants Chattanooga to secede from the state of Tennessee?"

"That's him. He's not the sharpest knife in the drawer."

I shuddered. "He seems like such a joke. I can't believe anyone would take him seriously."

"His father was a well-respected judge and senator. So he's got name recognition, looks, money, and a political machine that will most likely get him to Washington."

"Even if people find out he was having an affair with Naomi Keller?"

Dixie pondered that for several moments. "I don't know. Folks here in the Bible Belt can be very conservative about things like adultery. It would definitely hurt if the affair became public knowledge." She frowned.

"What's wrong?"

"I had heard rumors about Naomi for years. In fact, I had heard she was involved with Dixon Vannover. He's a real sleazeball. Honestly, he's just so snooty. I hate the way he's always looking down on people, like he's so much smarter. I worked on the board of the Chattanooga Council of the Arts, and he was so obnoxious, no one wanted to work with him."

"How long ago was it that you'd heard he and Naomi were . . . involved?"

Dixie thought for a few moments. "It wasn't that long, maybe a couple weeks."

"Let's put his name on the list," David said. "What about the injured spouses?"

"June Vannover and Warren Keller," Dixie said.

"June was furious at Naomi Keller," I said. "She threatened her too. Red heard her. Although, while I was furious at my husband, Albert, when I first found out he had been having an affair, I didn't kill him."

"What about Warren Keller?" David asked. "How would he feel about his wife fooling around with another man?"

Dixie shrugged.

I looked at my friend. "You don't like him."

"I don't. He's always struck me as a rather cold fish. I guess I don't like people who profit off other people's unhappiness." She thought for a minute. "It's not just that he's a lawyer who specializes in divorce; it's that he . . . seems to enjoy it too much. That's probably not fair. I'm just biased because I've known some couples that were going through rough times. I thought with time and support, they could have worked through it, but then Warren Keller got involved, and that was it." She shook her head. "Honestly, I think if Warren found out that his wife was having an affair, he'd probably volunteer to represent June and then take Dixon and Naomi for every penny they had."

We talked through our suspects but didn't have any other names that we could add to the list. That's when the doorbell rang.

David volunteered to get it, and he wasn't gone long when he came back with Monica Jill and B.J.

"How are you doing?" I asked Monica Jill.

"I'm perfectly fine, thank you very much, although some people," she tilted her head in B.J.'s direction, "don't believe me."

B.J. flopped down in a seat. "Nope. Some people sure don't believe it, and *some people* ain't taking no chances. You better be thankful I picked you up."

Monica Jill mumbled, "Prison guard."

"What was that?"

"Nothing," Monica Jill said, smiling.

B.J. went inside to take advantage of the facilities, and Monica Jill leaned forward. "Seriously, she is worse than a prison guard. You two have got to help me."

I chuckled. "Frankly, I don't see why you couldn't just stand up to her and tell her that you're an adult and you'll drive yourself."

"I tried, but when she took me home yesterday, she not only told my husband, but my mom was there, and do you know she actually told my mother?" Monica Jill stared from Dixie to me. "I could have convinced Zach that I was perfectly okay to drive, but I couldn't go up against all three of them."

"I still don't understand why you couldn't just . . . well, slip out."

She sighed. "Zach confiscated my keys."

We tried to hold it in, but eventually we all burst out laughing.

"I'm glad y'all think this so funny," Monica Jill said, giving us a hard stare. "The only thing that kept my husband from taking me to the emergency room was my promise to take it easy and not drive."

B.J. rejoined us. "And I plan on helping you keep that promise."

Monica Jill stuck out her tongue.

B.J. glanced at the notepad David had opened. "That looks like a suspect list to me." She turned to Monica Jill. "I told you Lilly wouldn't be able to resist finding a murderer. Housewarming or no housewarming."

Monica Jill clapped and gave me a big smile. "I'm so happy for you. Meeting his family is the first step. Next thing you know . . ." She held up her left hand and pointed at her ring finger.

I didn't need a mirror to know that I was blushing. I glanced over at David, who was also grinning. "Let's not count our eggs before they're hatched."

Red came around the side of the house.

B.J. mumbled, "Here comes the rooster now."

I kicked her under the table and turned to greet Red.

He gave me a kiss on the cheek. "Am I interrupting anything?"

"Nope," David said. "We were just talking about our next steps." He smoothly turned over his notepad as he stood and shook hands with Red. The gesture was subtle, but I knew from experience that little escaped Red's notice.

Red glanced around the table. "If I didn't know better, I'd think you all were investigating something."

"Actually, we were planning a housewarming party," Dixie said. She scooted over so Red could sit next to me. "Now, am I to understand you have five sisters?"

"Yep. I'm the youngest."

"Tell us about them. What do they do?"

Red didn't like being grilled and squirmed a bit. "My oldest sister is Mary. She's an ob/gyn. Then there's Sarah."

"She's the lawyer, right?" I asked.

"Yep. She has her own law firm in town." He took a deep breath. "Next is Catherine. She's a high school English teacher. Barbara is a real estate investor, and Amy—"

"Wait, your sister isn't Barbara Westfield, is she?" Monica Jill said, leaning forward.

"Westfield's her married name."

"Oh my God. I know her. She's the person that bought up all those rundown buildings in downtown Chattanooga and has been renovating them."

"Her husband owns Westfield Construction."

Monica Jill turned to Dixie. "That's who owns the building I told you would be perfect for your doggie day care, boarding, and grooming business."

Red looked confused. "I didn't know you were planning to start a business."

Dixie sipped her wine. "Neither did I."

Monica Jill huffed. "I think it would be perfect. People who work downtown could drop their dogs off on their way to work and pick them up afterward." She got more excited and animated as she spoke. "And the building is right across the street from the Choo-Choo Hotel, which doesn't take pets, but if Dixie had a day care and boarding facility, then tourists could just drop their dogs off." She stared at Red. "I've been trying to talk to your sister, but we keep playing phone tag. Is she going to be at the housewarming?"

Red nodded.

Monica Jill leaned back in her chair. "Fantastic."

"You have one more sister," I said. "That's only four."

"Amy is my youngest sister. She owns a hair salon."

"They're all so accomplished." I tried to sound confident, but I suspect the terror came through because Red reached under the table and squeezed my hand.

"They'll love you." He smiled. "They'll pump you like a flat tire, but they will love you." He leaned across and kissed me.

"What's not to love?" Dixie said. She smiled and sipped her wine.

"This is going to be great," Monica Jill said. "I can hardly wait. Now, what are we going to serve? And speaking of food, I'm starving."

"What is that delicious aroma?" B.J. asked.

I got up. "I put a roast in the crockpot. There was a sale on them at the Fresh Market, buy one, get one. I made French dip sandwiches with one and I thought I'd make a Mississippi pot roast with the other one. Give me a few minutes, and I'll bring it out."

"Want some help?" Red asked.

Red loved to cook, so I let him shred the meat and peppers and put it all on a platter while I made a salad and grabbed a couple more bottles of wine.

"You don't need to be nervous," Red said. "My family already thinks you're pretty special."

I stopped tossing the salad. "How can they? They've never met me."

"Apparently, you've done wonders for my 'surly disposition,' according to Mary, my oldest sister."

"How can they tell?"

"Very funny." He pulled me into an embrace and kissed me. "Actually, I can tell a difference. I feel happier."

I smiled. "Maybe you've found your happy place too."

He kissed me again. "I think I have."

Dixie came in the kitchen. "Sorry to break up this love fest, but the natives are hungry and getting restless."

Red took the platter outside. I directed Dixie to get more wineglasses and the bottles of wine, and I took the salad outside.

Mississippi pot roast was one of my favorite easy meals, and everyone enjoyed it. When we finished eating, David's phone rang, and I saw Madison's picture pop up on the screen before he grabbed it and excused himself. He wasn't gone long.

"I hope you don't mind, but I invited Madison to come over."

"Of course, I don't mind." I smiled. "I'm surprised you didn't invite her sooner."

"She said she had to work. The TBI is understaffed, and she volunteered for overtime. She's got some crazy idea about buying into a doggie day care business." He glanced from Dixie to Monica Jill.

Dixie was momentarily shocked, and Monica Jill was looking everywhere except at David and Dixie. When she wasn't able to avoid their gazes any longer, she said, "Okay, I might have mentioned something about the doggie day care being a great investment. And I may even have mentioned that I thought it would be a great business opportunity and that, if we all kicked in, we could go into this together." She looked sheepishly at Dixie. "I might even have mentioned that maybe Dixie could hire her to work nights and weekends."

Dixie's eyes got wide as a half-dollar. "Dixie could hire her? How am I supposed to hire anyone? I just mentioned that I had *thought* about opening a doggie day care. I never said I was absolutely going to do it."

Monica Jill's shoulder's slumped, and she looked up at Dixie with sad, puppy-dog eyes. "I know, but it was a really good idea."

Dixie sighed. "It's okay. It was . . . is a good idea. I can't say I haven't been thinking about it."

Monica Jill sat up and clapped. "I knew it." She whipped out her cell phone. After a few swipes, she found what she was looking for and held the phone out so we could see.

Everyone crowded around and looked at the pictures of the building she had found.

It was brick and located on Market Street, almost directly across the street from the Choo-Choo Hotel. Unlike most of the buildings on the street, this one was a stand-alone, not connected to other buildings. As she swiped to show all the pictures, Monica Jill excitedly shared all the building's strong points, along with her vision for what the finished product would look like.

"The location is awesome," Monica Jill said. "It has so much potential."

"Is that a tree growing through the roof?" B.J. asked.

"The building has been vacant for over ten years, so, yes, that's a tree, but you just need to look beyond the tree and check out the potential."

"Is that the price?" Dixie pointed at the screen. "That's outrageous. Tree or no tree. I don't have that kind of money for a rundown building with no grass for the dogs to run and play and that needs a complete gut job."

Monica Jill turned to Red. "Maybe we know someone who could get us a deal."

Red held up his hands. "I have a rule. I stay out of my sisters' businesses, and they stay out of mine."

Monica Jill stared at the faces of everyone around her. "But it's such a great location, and with investors and . . ."

Dixie, Red, B.J., and I all shook our heads.

"But if everyone chipped in, then it wouldn't—"

"I'm sorry to disappoint you," Dixie said, "but buying a business and opening a doggie day care would be stressful enough without the added pressure of having a derelict building that needs to be completely renovated. I wouldn't want to take the risk myself. I certainly wouldn't allow my friends to risk their hard-earned money as part of the bargain." Dixie folded her arms across her chest. "Absolutely not." She gave Monica Jill a long gaze and then her face softened. "I'm really sorry. I know you were excited, and you put a lot of work into this, but it's just . . . not the right time."

Monica Jill returned her phone to her purse. "It's okay. I understand."

The doorbell rang, and David hopped up to answer it. "That's probably Madison."

We scooted one of the extra chairs to my large patio set next to David's. When they returned, they both sat down. Madison had a large bag, which she placed on the table.

After the greetings were completed, she said, "I grabbed a burger before I left work, but I thought you all might want dessert." She pulled a pink box from the bag. I immediately recognized Nothing Bundt Cakes' distinctive packaging. She had brought a box of twelve cupcakes the bakery called "bundtinis."

We made short work of the delicious cakes.

After a few minutes, Red got a phone call and excused himself. He went inside and took the call in private.

When he was gone, Madison leaned forward. "Listen, if that call is what I think it is, then, Mrs. Jefferson, you may not have much time."

Dixie looked shocked. "What?"

"When I was leaving work, I overheard the director talking." She glanced around to make sure Red hadn't returned. "I only heard one side of the conversation, and I didn't hear everything that was said, but I could tell he was being pressured to make an arrest."

Dixie went pale. "You don't mean they intend to arrest me?"

Madison didn't reply, but her silence confirmed Dixie's question.

"Oh my God. This is a nightmare."

"Who was the call from?" I asked. "Who could have that much pull to call the director of the Tennessee Bureau of Investigation on a Sunday and demand an arrest?"

She shook her head. "I have no idea, but I don't think he wanted to do it. He seemed . . . annoyed."

Dixie put her head in her hands. "What am I going to do?"

"Well, the first thing you're going to do is stop acting helpless," B.J. ordered.

The shock of her statement worked like cold water to help snap Dixie out of her mood. "You're right."

"Now, pick up your phone and call your husband and get your attorney." B.J. turned to me. "Did you say your daughter was coming?"

"She's in Nashville at a conference. I was going to drive to Nashville to pick up Lucky and then when the conference was over, she was coming here for a few days, but I'm sure she'd come early and help." I picked up my cell phone and called my daughter.

By the time Red came back outside, we had all concluded our calls. Red looked angrier than I'd ever seen him. He clenched his jaw, and the vein on the side of his head pulsed and caused blood to rush to the scar on the side of his face, making it look even more raised and inflamed. "Dixie, I'm sorry, but I just learned they're sending someone to pick you up in connection with the murder of Naomi Keller." He paused. "I'm terribly sorry, but—"

"Can you take me in?" Dixie asked.

Red stared. "What?"

"Do I have to wait to be arrested? Or can you take me to the police station or the TBI offices or wherever?" Dixie reached out her hand and touched his arm. "If I'm going to be arrested, I'd much rather you did it."

The two stared at each other. Eventually, Red nodded.

When the shock wore off, we went into action. I turned to Madison. "Stephanie was at the airport in Chicago. Her flight will land in Nashville in two hours. Can you and David—"

David hopped up. "Absolutely."

"I'll text you the airline and flight information, but you two better hit the road."

David and Madison hurried out.

I glanced at B.J. and Monica Jill. "I'm going to follow Red to the station and wait for Beau."

"What can we do?" B.J. and Monica Jill asked.

My cell phone vibrated with a text message. "This is from Beau. He's taking the next flight back to Chattanooga but wants to know if someone can pick him up at the airport. Or take Dixie's car and leave it for him? He has his own keys." I opened Dixie's purse and pulled out her car keys. "Can one of you . . ."

Monica Jill snatched the keys from my hands. "Absolutely." Before B.J. could protest, she said, "I'll drive your car, and B.J. can follow me. We'll leave the car at the airport for Beau." She glanced at B.J., who nodded her agreement.

The two of them hurried away, leaving me alone in the backyard. I scooped up Aggie and Rex and took them inside. I said a quick prayer and then hurried after Red and Dixie. What had started out as a good day had quickly hit my top five worst days ever. I knew Dixie hadn't murdered Naomi Keller, but I also knew that innocence didn't guarantee freedom, especially if someone was determined to hang the murder around Dixie's neck. No, it would take innocence and the use of every one of my little gray cells, not to mention lots of luck, to get my friend out of this one.

Chapter 9

I pulled into the TBI parking lot, which was located in a business park not far from my old rental home. I was relieved when Red sent me a text that he was taking Dixie here rather than down to the police station for questioning. I'm sure he wanted to spare her the embarrassment of being taken to the police station, although I wasn't sure how his superiors would take it.

The Chattanooga TBI office was just a small brick building that resembled a post office more than a law enforcement agency. However, it was still not the way that Dixie would want to spend her Sunday.

There weren't a lot of cars in the lot, but I did notice a black-and-white police car and knew that the officer leading the investigation was there. When I got to the door, I saw Red, Dixie, and another man standing in the lobby. Based on his military haircut, his authoritative stance, and the gun strapped to his waist, I knew he must be a plainclothes police officer.

Red opened the door and winked. He turned to the officers. "Mrs. Echosby is here as a witness."

The man turned and stared at me. "Witness?"

"Officer Lewis." I extended my hand. "Nice to see you again . . . although I wish it were under different circumstances."

Officer Lewis shook my hand, but his eyes indicated he too would have preferred any circumstances other than a murder investigation. "Mrs. Echosby, I'm surprised to see you here."

Officer Lewis had been the investigating officer when Aggie dug up a dead body. He was with the Chattanooga Police Department, and I tried not to hold it against him that he thought I'd murdered the man. In the end, when the real murderer was identified, we'd buried the hatchet that had made us opponents rather than friends. He was a light-skinned African American man with light gray eyes, which were looking skeptically at me before he flashed them at Red.

"I should have known when they told me you specifically asked to work with me that you had something up your sleeve."

"Hey, all I said was that I wanted to work with the best investigator the CPD had." He spread his arms wide and shrugged. "How was I supposed to know they'd send you?"

The two men stared at each other for a few seconds, and then Officer Lewis shook his head and sighed. "Okay, I see how this is going to go." He gave Red an intense stare. "What do you want?"

"All I want is an intelligent investigator—"

"You can cut the flattery. If I remember correctly, you didn't think much of my intelligence when I was investigating your girlfriend here."

Red smiled. "Water under the bridge. I just need you to keep an open mind and—"

"Keep an open mind, and sit back, and let Nancy Drew here solve the mystery and find the murderer?"

Red must have known that I wouldn't take kindly to the Nancy Drew reference because he shot me a glance that said *Let me handle this* before any words could leave my mouth. "Look, we both know that Officer Dan Martin has the finesse of a freight train."

Lewis grudgingly nodded.

"Besides, Lilly did help catch a murderer. Actually, she's solved several murders and saved the CPD from some embarrassing arrests." He rubbed the back of his neck. "Look, I know how it looks, but I've also come to know . . . and love these people. Dixie didn't murder Naomi Keller, and regardless of what you or I or any law enforcement officer does, I also know that Lilly Echosby will move heaven and earth to prove it. She *will* find the real killer."

It took everything in me not to throw my arms around his neck and kiss him in the lobby of the TBI office. Instead, I wiped the tears that threatened to leave me a blubbering baby from my eyes and tried to look dignified and . . . sleuth-ish.

Officer Lewis glanced from Red to me and eventually shrugged. "Alright."

The two men stared at each other and came to some type of manly, law-enforcement, telepathic understanding, which reached completion when they both gave the slightest of nods.

Red's posture relaxed. "Thanks. I owe you one." He turned to escort Officer Lewis down the hall. When he noticed I was following, he turned and said, "Sorry, but you're going to need to wait here in the lobby."

I sat and waited. My brain was in overdrive, so I didn't wait patiently. From time to time, I stood up and paced. When I was tired of pacing, I sat until I was tired of that, and then I paced some more. Half an hour later, Monica Jill and B.J. arrived. And we waited. Time stood still, or at least it felt like it. Eventually, Beau arrived. He looked wild-eyed but relaxed a mite when he saw me. We hugged.

"Where is she?"

"She's in a room with Red and Officer Lewis from the Chattanooga Police."

He ran his hand through his hair. "She shouldn't be in there alone."

"I got a text message from Red that Dixie's lawyer was there."

He released the breath he'd been holding. "I'm her husband. I should be in there with her."

"I don't think that's how this works." I tried to reassure him. "Stephanie sent her a text message not to say a word without legal counsel. I'm sure she'll be fine," I said, with more confidence than I felt.

I looked up and was surprised when Dr. Morgan and Mai Nguyen arrived. We had met Mai a few months ago, and she and Dr. Morgan had been dating ever since. Mai was five feet tall and petite with long dark hair.

"What are you two doing here?" I asked.

"B.J. sent us a text message that Dixie was in trouble."

"Well, I figured the more the merrier," B.J. said, "especially if we needed to stage a breakout."

"You can't joke like that," Monica Jill said. She glanced around and then whispered, "We're at the TBI. They probably have this entire place bugged and videotaped. We won't be able to help Dixie if we all end up getting arrested."

I couldn't help myself from looking around and noticing all the cameras. However, I doubted that the facility was bugged, but I'd be sure to ask Red later.

Beau paced like a wild tiger in a cage, ready to pounce any time he heard a noise.

I glanced at my phone and noted the time. I'd been there for two hours. I was just about to suggest someone go for coffee when I heard footsteps.

Red, Dixie, Officer Lewis, and a man I didn't recognize came around the corner.

Beau rushed to Dixie and wrapped her in his arms.

We waited for a few moments before interrupting.

"Dixie, are you okay?" Monica Jill asked.

B.J. glared from Officer Lewis to Red. "'Cause, if they tried to railroad you, we can get the news media down here real quick."

Dixie smiled. "I'm fine. Although I'm rather surprised and touched to see all of you." She wiped away a tear and nodded. "They just asked a few questions." She turned back to the man who was standing behind her. "This is my attorney, Theodore Jordan. Theodore, these are my friends."

Theodore Jordan was a tall, handsome African American man who looked to be in his early seventies with salt-and-pepper hair. He shook hands with each of us.

Beau put his arm around Dixie's shoulder. "Let's go home. You can fill me in there." He shook Theodore Jordan's hand again. "Thank you for dropping everything and coming out so quickly on short notice."

Theodore smiled. "No problem. I'll let you two get some rest and come by tomorrow, and we can talk more." He turned and nodded to Officer Lewis and Red. "Gentlemen."

They nodded.

We all went outside. Before getting into our respective cars, Dixie turned to face everyone. "I really am fine." She reached out and squeezed my hand. "Red and Officer Lewis were extremely courteous."

I relaxed a bit. I loved Red, but I also loved Dixie. She was my best friend. The biggest struggle I faced while waiting in that lobby was the internal one going through my mind. I'd heard about the blue wall and how law-enforcement officers stuck together. What if Red was forced to arrest my best friend? As much as I cared about him, it would hurt knowing that he would arrest someone he felt was innocent, someone he knows. Fortunately, he'd managed to avoid actually arresting her . . . for now. But what if he was ordered to arrest her? I knew in my head that he would only be doing his job. However, my heart was struggling. It didn't make sense, but I still had idealistic expectations that the police should be more interested in finding the *right* person than in merely arresting someone they knew was innocent. Sure, it was his job, but that idea was the excuse used in the Nuremberg defense in World War II. *I was only following orders.* I knew this situation wasn't on the same scale as Nuremberg, but I firmly believed that men of character, especially men in positions of authority, wouldn't simply follow orders. I'd grown up with the belief that there was *no right way to do a wrong thing.* If he believed Dixie to be guilty, then arresting her would be the right thing, but I knew he didn't. These were the thoughts that had tortured me for the past few hours, and I still didn't have an answer to them.

"I want to thank all of you for taking such good care of my Dixie," Beau said, choking on his emotions. After a moment, he swallowed hard and continued. "Please, let us provide dinner for everyone tomorrow at our house."

Everyone nodded their agreement.

Dixie leaned close and whispered, "I can come get you. I know you don't like driving up Lookout Mountain."

"It's okay. I'm sure David will love it. Worst-case scenario, I'll drive to the bottom of the mountain, and you can come get us."

I glanced back at the building before getting in the car. Red and Officer Lewis were still inside. I had the drive home to think about Naomi Keller, Dixie, Red, and murder. By the time I arrived, I decided the only thing to do was to find Naomi Keller's murderer before I was forced to make a choice between my boyfriend and my best friend.

Chapter 10

An accident on Interstate 24 had traffic backed up for miles, and it was dark before David and Madison arrived with Stephanie and Lucky. I was ecstatic to see my daughter, and Aggie and Rex were equally ecstatic to see Lucky.

After a quick recap of events, Madison said she had an early day tomorrow and went home, leaving David, Stephanie, and me to catch up. Hours in the car had provided plenty of time for David and Madison to fill Stephanie in on everything they knew, so there really wasn't much left to tell. Stephanie looked exhausted after a day of travel, so we kept things short and went to bed.

Aggie, Rex, and I settled into bed and were just about to call it a night when I got a text from Red asking if everything was okay. I started a reply several times before finally typing, *It will be.* I could see he was struggling with what to say and eventually ended with, *I love you.* It didn't take me nearly as long to type, *I love you too.* When there was no other message, I plugged my phone in to the charger and grabbed a notepad.

I quickly read through the notes David had taken earlier. Hard to believe that it was only a few hours ago that we had sat on the back deck, sipping wine and coming up with suspects for Naomi Keller's murder.

Brittney Keller hated her stepmother. She humiliated her at a dog show. However, humiliation and murder were two separate things. Did Brittney hate Naomi Keller enough to murder her?

June Vannover was jealous, and she said she hated Naomi Keller. There was a part of me that empathized with her. I knew what it was like to feel tossed aside by the man you loved—the man you'd pledged your troth to. There were certainly times when I wanted to kill Bambi, the bimbo I blamed for wrecking my marriage. Of course, time had helped me realize that Bambi wasn't solely to blame. June wasn't ready to accept that yet. She could certainly have believed that if she killed Naomi Keller, then all would go back to normal with her marriage. The question is, did she do it? Did she kill her rival for her husband's affection?

What about the injured spouses? Was Warren Keller aware that his wife had been having an affair and planned to leave him? If he did, did he care? Would he care enough to murder her? Would Dixon Vannover have a motive? If Naomi Keller had tired of Dixon Vannover, maybe he killed her?

Tomorrow, we would need to divide and conquer. We needed to figure out which one of these suspects killed Naomi Keller, and we needed to do it quickly. Someone had pressured the head of the TBI to pick up Dixie. Who had that type of pull? Red had prevented an actual arrest, but he wouldn't be able to do that for long. If we didn't provide another viable suspect soon, he could be forced to arrest her. If he refused, they would simply remove him from the case and make someone else do it. We would need to move quickly to find Naomi Keller's murderer.

Chapter 11

I was up early the next morning but found that Stephanie and David had both beat me and were sitting outside sipping coffee on the back deck. I opened the door and let Aggie and Rex outside and then poured a cup of coffee and joined them.

"Have you two been up long?"

Stephanie and David both shook their heads.

"I couldn't stop thinking about Aunt Dixie," Stephanie said, "so I got up."

David sipped his coffee. "Me too." He looked at me. "Is there anything either of us can do before the meeting tonight?"

I was so proud of the caring adults my children had become. I thought for a minute and then turned to David. "I was thinking about that too. Dixon Vannover was having an affair with Naomi Keller. He's running for office, and I was wondering if you could swing by his campaign headquarters and volunteer to stuff envelopes or something and talk to a few of the workers. Surely, someone must have heard or seen something."

"My political sensibilities might chafe, but I'll do it."

Stephanie turned to me. "What about me? Aunt Dixie has an attorney, so he may not want me mucking about."

I waved that away. "He seemed like a nice man, and even though you're not licensed in Tennessee, I'm sure Dixie will want you to be involved." I paused.

"What?" Stephanie said, leaning forward. "I know that look. You have something up your sleeve. Spill it."

"Naomi Keller's husband, Warren, was a divorce attorney. I don't know where attorneys hang out, but maybe Theodore Jordan, Dixie's attorney, can point you in the right direction."

Stephanie smiled. "If there's a restaurant near the courthouse or, better yet, a bar, then I'm sure I'll find out all the dirt on Warren Keller there is to find."

"There's a bar, but there's also a small restaurant that has the best barbecue I've ever eaten. It's run by a former football player, Moose Mitchell, and his wife, Renee."

"Sounds great." Stephanie smiled. "What about you? I know you have to work, but I find it hard to believe that you're going to leave all of the sleuthing to us."

"I'm going to find out what I can about Dixon Vannover. He's on the board of the museum, and Linda Kay and Jacob will be able to provide some of the information I need."

I finished my coffee and hurried to shower and dress, leaving Aggie and Rex outside with Lucky.

David dropped me off in the Arts District downtown at Da Vinci's, the bakery nearest the Chattanooga Museum of Art, which is where I worked. Jacob and Linda Kay wouldn't need buttering up to spill the beans on Dixon Vannover, but pastries from Da Vinci's, along with some tea, would certainly keep the conversation going. Before he left, I reminded David that he would need him to pick me up and confirmed that he was up to the task of driving up Lookout Mountain. Part of my heart raced when I realized how excited he was about what I considered a harrowing ascent.

Pastries in hand, I walked into the museum and placed the box on the desk of Jacob Fleming. Jacob was the assistant to the executive director, Linda Kay Weyman. He was in his early twenties, thin, with dark eyes and dark curly hair, which he wore pulled back into a man bun. As always, he was stylishly dressed, with red, rectangular glasses, black skinny jeans, and a black cashmere sweater.

Jacob had unlocked my office door and opened my curtains so I could sit and enjoy the view of the Tennessee River for several minutes before starting my day. I loved working at the museum. The Chattanooga Museum of Art was founded by the Hopewell family and funded through a trust. Linda Kay and Jacob were full-time employees. I had been hired as a temp to straighten out the museum's finances after the board hired an incompetent Hopewell family member as their accountant. As a temp, I knew my assignment could end at the board's whim, although I tried not to dwell on that possibility. Nevertheless, it loomed over my thoughts, especially today, because I knew saving Dixie might mean antagonizing one of the board members who held my future in his hands. If Dixon Vannover wanted to, he could fire me or simply cancel my assignment. If he were involved in Naomi Keller's murder, saving my best friend could jeopardize my future in more ways than one.

Chapter 12

Jacob popped his head in my office about thirty minutes later, letting me know Linda Kay had arrived. One of the advantages of working at a museum was there were lots of beautiful pieces of art all around me. However, Linda Kay wasn't just the executive director of an art museum; she was an art connoisseur and collector. Her office, like her home, was full of beautiful paintings, vases, fine china, and other wonderful pieces. The incredible thing about Linda Kay was that she believed in using objects for the purposes for which they were created, so when I entered her office, I wasn't surprised to see that Jacob had taken the pastries out of the box and had them displayed on a blue and white Blue Willow china set. I knew the set was one of her favorites and had belonged to her grandmother.

"Good morning," Linda Kay said, beaming. "I've been so anxious to hear about Naomi Keller's death that I nearly called you over the weekend. What on earth happened?"

Linda Kay was a middle-aged Southern belle. She had red hair, bright eyes, a warm smile, and a razor-sharp mind. When she was behind her desk, you couldn't tell that she only had one leg, but she slid from her chair to her scooter and then motored over to the conference table.

My office was large and directly next door to Linda Kay's, whose office was massive in comparison. She had room not only for a desk but also a conference table and six chairs in the section where she hosted meetings.

I gave her and Jacob the details from the dog show and recounted the attempt to get Dixie arrested for the murder.

Linda Kay gasped. "Well, they can't do that. Anybody with the sense God gave a grasshopper would know that Dixie couldn't hurt a fly."

"Well, I know Dixie didn't murder her, but the fact she not only argued with Naomi but also punched her didn't look good."

Linda Kay chuckled. "I wish I'd been there to see that."

I tried not to grin, but I couldn't control the corners of my mouth. "It was pretty funny. But Dixie can't be the only person who wanted to deck Naomi Keller. I only just met her on Saturday, but she was definitely abrasive."

"Abrasive is an understatement," Jacob said.

"There have to be plenty of people who had a reason to kill Naomi Keller. Can either of you think of anyone?"

Jacob and Linda Kay exchanged glances.

"What?"

Linda Kay leaned closer. "I don't like to spread gossip, but I had heard there was some hanky-panky going on with that Keller girl and Dixon Vannover."

I tried not to allow my confusion to show, but I'd just shared that June Vannover had confirmed that her husband was having an affair, so I was confused about why this had generated the looks they'd just exchanged. "As I said, June did say her husband and Naomi were having an affair, but—"

Jacob waved his hand as though erasing a blackboard. "Not Naomi, Brittney . . . Brittney Keller."

It was my turn to gasp. "You mean Dixon Vannover was having an affair with both of them? With Brittney Keller and her stepmother?"

They both nodded.

"But that's . . . I mean, how long ago was that? It couldn't have been recent? Could it?"

Jacob bit into his pastry. "I heard about it a couple of months ago, which is a lifetime when you're dealing with a womanizer like Vannover."

"Surely, he wouldn't have an affair with both women at the same time, right?" For some reason, I found myself whispering, as though someone would hear this dirty secret.

Linda Kay shrugged. "I wouldn't put it past that little weasel."

There was no love lost between Linda Kay and Dixon Vannover, but I still couldn't believe anyone capable of that. "I know he's ambitious and arrogant, but—"

"Ambitious?" Linda Kay put her cup down and turned to stare at me. "That man would stop at nothing to move up the ladder. He'd sell out his grandmother if he thought it would get him to Washington."

"Adultery is bad enough. Trust me, I know, but this is ten times worse. Cheating on your spouse with a mother *and* daughter is a completely different level of sleaziness."

"Technically, it's her stepdaughter," Jacob said, "but that doesn't really make it better."

Linda Kay and I said together, "No, it doesn't."

I tried to push my emotions aside and think objectively. "If Brittney had found out about her stepmother and her boyfriend, that might have given her a stronger motive for murder."

Linda Kay nodded. "Indeed, it would."

We chatted a little longer, but Linda Kay had to get to a meeting, and I had work to do too. David called to see if I wanted him to pick me up for lunch, but I was neck-deep in figures, trying to make sure everything was perfect for the upcoming board meeting, so I told him I'd grab something from the cafeteria.

After work, I was picked up by David, Stephanie, and three dogs. My office was closer to Lookout Mountain, so I had packed a bag with casual clothes and shoes and planned to change at Dixie's house. When they arrived, Stephanie opened the door to move to the back seat and allow me to ride up front, but I stopped her.

"I'd much prefer to ride on the back seat with the dogs, where I can see less of the ascent up that mountain."

Stephanie got back into the car, and David did a poor job of hiding his smile. Eventually, he allowed himself to laugh out loud, but I didn't care.

"Laugh all you want." I slammed the back door and buckled myself in.

I spent the ride up the mountain with my eyes closed, rosary in hand, and Aggie clutched to my chest. When the car finally stopped, I pried one eye open enough to make sure we were at the top at last. I said a prayer of thanks, wiped the sweat from my forehead, and opened the door.

The view from atop Lookout Mountain was spectacular, but I was still in no shape to enjoy it. Experience told me it would take at least thirty minutes and a glass of wine before I was calm enough to soak it in. Prior to moving to Chattanooga, I had no idea that heights were a problem for me. Indiana was flat, so I hadn't known how terrified I was of heights until Dixie took me to her house for the first time. Usually, she or Beau would drive whenever I needed to come, or I'd drive to the base of the mountain and one of them would come down and get me. However, David's travels had taken him to France and Switzerland, and he was not only adept at mountain driving, he enjoyed it.

I recognized several of the cars parked in front of Dixie's house and knew that Monica Jill, B.J., and Dr. Morgan had already arrived. There was also a black BMW that I didn't recognize. However, when we went inside, I saw Theodore Jordan drinking a beer with Beau and knew the Bimmer belonged to him.

Dixie greeted us and gave Stephanie a tight squeeze. "I'm so glad you came. I know you can't represent me, but . . . I just feel better knowing you're here."

"I'm happy to help any way I can," Stephanie whispered. "I hope you don't mind, but I looked up Theodore Jordan and asked around, and he has a really good reputation."

"Of course I don't mind." Dixie hugged her. "Thank you."

Once I got over the stress of the drive up the mountain and my nerves settled down, I always enjoyed walking through Dixie's home. It was gorgeous. Dixie and Beau had a large, sprawling estate atop Lookout Mountain that provided a spectacular vista over the city. The house was a Frank Lloyd Wright–inspired design, with three bedrooms and four baths. It was larger than it appeared from the front, with over 3,000 square feet of floor space. Guests entered on the main level. The back of the house had a broad wall of windows that overlooked the city of Chattanooga and the Tennessee River. However, the entertaining happened on the lower level, which included a swimming pool and a large stone deck for enjoying the million-dollar views.

When we went downstairs, I caught sight of Catherine Huntington, Dixie's cook, placing a large platter of food onto a table that was already overladen. Catherine was a large-boned woman with gray hair, which she pulled back into a bun. She had a plain face, but when she saw me, she lit up and was transformed. Instead of plain and homely, she was intelligent and kind. Catherine Huntington had spent many years working for a wealthy Scotsman, but when he was murdered, she found herself in a precarious situation. Dixie and I were able to help her not only find a new job; she also credited us with saving her life, which technically, we did. She was extremely grateful.

"I'm so happy to see you again, Mrs. Echosby." She hugged me and beamed. Then she turned to Stephanie. "And you've brought your beautiful daughter."

"I don't think you've met my son." I beckoned for David to come over. "This is my son, David."

She gaped at him and then grabbed his hand and pumped it as she shook. "You're such a handsome young man, so like your mother." She leaned close. "I'll bet you have left a string of broken hearts all over the country."

David smiled. "Not as many as you'd think."

"I cooked enough food to feed an army, but if there's anything you want, you just let me know. I'll be happy to get it."

We complimented her on the food, which was truly a feast for the eyes and smelled wonderful too, and then we assured her that if we needed anything, no matter how small, we'd let her know. With that promise, she hurried upstairs to bring down more, although I wasn't sure where she'd put the dishes.

Dixie whispered, "She's been cooking practically all night, especially when she found out you were coming."

"What are you going to do with all of this? Unless you've invited your entire neighborhood to join us, there's no way we can eat all this food."

B.J. came up behind me. "Well, I'm sure going to do my best to take as much of this off your hands as I can." She piled chicken wings on top of ribs and an already full plate.

"Honestly, I wasn't sure that Beau and I needed a cook." Dixie smiled. "After all, it's just the two of us and two poodles, but she's been wonderful. She cooks and cleans and does laundry." She glanced at her husband, who was talking to Dr. Morgan and Mai Nguyen. "Plus, I think Beau's cholesterol is much better since she's been cooking heart-healthy meals."

"You call ribs, chicken, roasts, and ham heart-healthy?" Monica Jill asked.

Dixie glanced at the table. "Today is an exception. Normally, we eat pretty light and a lot healthier, but I let her have her way and cook whatever she wanted." She grinned at me. "As long as it didn't involve kidneys, hearts, or other organs."

"It certainly looks a lot better than the haggis we had the last time I was here," Stephanie said.

"Technically, she didn't cook that," I reminded her.

I noticed all the chairs were arranged in a circle and turned to Dixie. "I was just joking when I said you would need to invite your neighborhood, but who else is coming?"

Dixie was about to respond when Red and Madison came down the stairs.

I turned to Dixie and whispered, "Are you sure you want them here?"

"Beau and I talked about it. I know Red's technically the enemy, but I trust him. He could have taken me to the police station, but he didn't. He could have turned me over to that troll who came the other day, but . . . he didn't." She sighed. "I decided to trust my instincts. They're family, and I trust both of them."

Red moved beside me. "Can we talk?"

I nodded, and we went down the hall to a room near the back of the house, where Dixie had set up her grooming table and equipment.

"Are you okay with me being here?"

"It's not my party. Dixie—"

"I'm not worried about Dixie right now. I'm talking about you. Are *you* okay with me being here? If you want me to leave, then I'll go, but I hope you know I would never do anything to deliberately hurt Dixie. I—"

I reached up and kissed him. He held me close, and I could feel his heart race. When we separated, he looked down at me, and I could see the strain on his face. "I know Dixie didn't murder anyone, and I promise you, I'll do everything I can to help." He reached in his pocket and pulled out his shield and handed it to me. "You're more important to me than anything else, including that. I need you to know I'm not here as a TBI officer. I'm here as a friend."

"I know." I reached inside his jacket and put his shield back where it belonged. "Let's get some food, and then we can put our heads together and figure out who murdered Naomi Keller and is trying to frame my friend . . . our friend."

Chapter 13

Dinner was delicious. We all ate and drank and had a great time talking about everything except the one subject that was paramount on everyone's minds. However, after dinner, we got down to business. By some unseen rule, everyone turned to me to lead the discussion.

"I guess we all know why we're here. So let's get started." I pulled out the notebook I'd stuffed in my purse earlier. "I'll kick things off." I shared the information that I had learned from Linda Kay and Jacob about the love triangle between Dixon Vannover, Naomi Keller, and Brittney. As I expected, everyone was shocked.

"Why, that dirty dog," B.J. said, taking another bite of cheesecake.

Monica Jill scowled. "He should be horse-whipped."

Red asked, "Do you think they knew about each other?"

"I'm not sure," I said. "But if Linda Kay and Jacob knew, then it couldn't have been much of a secret, could it?"

We gnawed on that piece of information until there was nothing left to say. Everyone agreed that Dixon Vannover was scum; however, that didn't make him a killer.

Dr. Morgan cleared his throat. "I managed to switch with someone, so I got assigned to the autopsy."

Mai gave him an adoring look. "That's so sweet."

Dr. Morgan blushed and hurried on. "Death was due to strangulation."

"We already knew that," Monica Jill said.

He smiled. "True, but I can also confirm that Naomi Keller was not pregnant."

"What?"

Dixie leaned forward. "Are you sure?"

He nodded.

I frowned. "But how is that possible? June Vannover said that's why Dixon was leaving her, because she couldn't have children and Naomi Keller was able to give him the one thing she couldn't."

"Could she have had a miscarriage?" Dixie asked.

Dr. Morgan shook his head. "She'd had a full hysterectomy."

We mulled that bombshell over for quite some time.

"So if Dixon Vannover found out that Naomi Keller had lied to him," David said, "he might have wanted to strangle her."

Red smiled. "He might indeed. I think I'll have a talk with Dixon Vannover."

David raised a hand. "I went by his campaign headquarters today to see if I could find out anything."

"Did you?" Madison asked.

He shook his head. "Dixon Vannover made a brief appearance, and he looked horrible. Unfortunately, I didn't get a chance to talk to him, and the aides I did talk to didn't have anything negative to say."

Something in his eyes made me ask, "But there was something?"

"It was strange. I can't put my finger on what's wrong, but there's definitely something wrong there."

"You mean other than the fact that the man is a total and complete idiot?" B.J. said.

"And a two-timing, adulterous letch," Monica Jill said.

"Yeah, other than that, he's perfectly normal." David smiled. "I'm going back tomorrow, so hopefully I'll be able to talk to a few more people and see what I can find out."

"Thank you, David," Dixie said.

Stephanie scooted to the front of her chair. "I went down to a pub near the courthouse, and Warren Keller is not well liked at all."

"Why not?" I asked.

"According to his secretary, the bartender, and one of the clerks from the courthouse, he's a bit cutthroat. In fact, they referred to him as a shark. He's very intelligent, but he uses his intelligence to intimidate others." She sat and thought for a few minutes. "He's really smart . . . probably has an IQ at the genius level, but he uses his intelligence like a weapon." She sighed. "I'm not explaining this well."

"Can you give us an example?" Red asked.

Theodore Jordan, who was sitting quietly in the corner, cleared his throat. "Maybe I can help."

We turned to watch the distinguished gentleman decide how best to say what he wanted. Beau gazed at his friend. "Teddy, you might as well spit it out. You're among friends, and nothing you say will ever get traced back to you."

The older lawyer leaned back and interlaced his fingers. After a few moments, he nodded at Stephanie. "Miss Echosby is right. Warren Keller is considered a shark. He's highly intelligent and very skilled. When he's arguing a point of law, if he thinks he's right, then he is relentless. He'll latch onto a point, and he won't let go."

"Isn't that the mark of a good attorney?" I asked, thinking of how persistent Stephanie was when she was pursuing justice.

Jordan smiled. "In certain situations, yes. In a courtroom, while arguing for truth and justice, then I would agree with you, but . . . most people have limitations, a line in the sand that we refuse to cross." He thought for a moment. "You know, a few years ago, I took a trip to Africa and went on a safari. I saw a lion hunting an injured gazelle. The lion watched the gazelles until it identified its prey. Then it culled the weaker animal, so it was isolated and alone. Only then did it take the wounded animal down." He paused and allowed his words to sink in. "Warren Keller is like that lion."

Despite my best efforts, I shivered.

"My guides explained that was the way of animals in the wild. It's the circle of life in action. Most human beings find that behavior distasteful. We don't prey on the poor, the infirm, or the weak. We root for the underdog. If someone has their back against the wall, we back off. It's considered . . . dishonorable to kick someone when they're down. Well, that's not Warren Keller's way. If he senses he has his prey backed up against the wall, if he senses fear, then he goes in for the kill. He goes for the jugular, and he won't let go until his enemy not only gives in but is totally and completely destroyed."

"Wow," B.J. said. "He sounds absolutely brutal."

Stephanie nodded. "That's essentially what I found out. Most people don't like him. However, he has an excellent track record in court. So if you can afford his exorbitant fees, then he practically guarantees results. He is going to win, regardless of his opponent."

"I thought you said he was a divorce attorney," Monica Jill asked, looking puzzled. "There are no winners when it comes to divorce."

We sat in silence, digesting this for several moments.

Stephanie took a deep breath. "I think Mr. Jordan summed up what I found very nicely." She smiled at Theodore Jordan, who nodded.

Red shook his head. "He sounds like a horrible human being, and if someone had murdered him, then the line of suspects is probably a mile long. Unfortunately, being a rotten person doesn't make him a killer. There are tons of evil people out there. I need some facts to go on."

"I don't have anyone who witnessed him strangling his wife," Stephanie said. "The only thing I can speak to is what I found about the man's character, which isn't very nice. However, I'm going to go back tomorrow and look for more."

David and Madison were whispering in a corner. "Madison?" I said. "Do you have anything to add?" I gave her my most encouraging smile.

She glanced tentatively at Red, who surprised her by saying, "Cooper, I think you understand this is all highly irregular and outside of TBI regulations. But as Beau mentioned earlier, we're all friends here, and we need to get to the bottom of this and find Naomi Keller's murderer, so if you have some information . . . please share."

"Well, I just happened to notice something about the body." She glanced at David, who gave her an encouraging nod. "It's just that it seemed odd to me that she was strangled with a lead, not a leash."

I frowned, trying to see why that was significant. "I'm sorry, dear, I don't—"

"Are you sure it was a lead?" Dixie moved forward in her seat.

Madison nodded.

The rest of us exchanged confused glances.

"You mentioned that the other day at the dog club," I said, "but I didn't understand what difference that made."

Monica Jill raised her hand tentatively. "I'm sorry, but I don't think I know the difference."

"Me either," B.J. added.

We turned to Dixie.

She got up and went through to the room where Red and I had talked earlier. She came back carrying two objects. One was clearly a short, six-foot leather dog leash with a clip on the end for connecting to a dog collar. She held it up. "This is a dog *leash*." She turned to one of her Standard Poodles, which was sprawled out at her feet. The dog stretched but then stood quietly while Dixie connected the leash to the dog's collar. "Most people use these."

"That's the type of leash we had to use in the obedience ring." Dr. Morgan said, giving the leash a hard look.

"Right." Dixie held up the other item. "This is a slip *lead*. It's a single line with a ring at one end." She fed the long end of the thin material through the ring so it formed a loop. "It makes a continuous loop, which you slide over the dog's head." She slipped the lead over the head of Leia, her other Standard Poodle. "A slip lead is the simplest way to control a dog." She demonstrated by doing a heel pattern with Leia. "The slip lead can easily adjust to the size of the dog's neck, making it virtually impossible for the dog to get out of it."

"Maybe that's what I need for Jac," Monica Jill said. "How does it work?"

Dixie slid the lead off Leia and held it up like a noose. "If the dog tries to go a different direction, the lead tightens and constricts and makes it uncomfortable."

"That seems rather cruel," Monica Jill whispered.

"Used in the right way, it's actually very safe. They're easy to get on and off, so it's great for dog training, but the placement is critical. The slip lead should sit high on the neck toward the ears to avoid causing the dog to cough or choke. It's a sensitive area, and dogs are less inclined to pull too hard."

Red shook his head. "Okay, but I don't understand why it matters. What difference does it make that Naomi Keller was strangled with a lead rather than a leash?"

I had been wondering the same thing, but I think I finally figured out why the lead was important. "This was an obedience show, not a confirmation show." I turned to glance at Dixie to see if I was right. She nodded. "The reason it matters is that American Kennel Club regulations require all dogs to wear a flat leather or fabric collar and use a fabric or leather leash."

"But this wasn't a real show," Red said. "This was just a mock trial."

I could see the light bulb go on for B.J. She snapped her fingers. "Since we were trying to simulate a real show with show conditions, everyone who was competing had collars on their dogs. And everyone I saw was using a leash." She pointed to the slip lead Dixie held. "Not a slip lead."

"So where did the lead that was used to strangle Naomi Keller come from?" Mai Nguyen asked.

We glanced around at each other.

"Could she have brought it?" Red asked, looking from me to Dixie.

Dixie shrugged. "She showed her Greyhounds in conformation, so it could have been one of hers."

"Which would indicate the murderer grabbed the closest object available."

"Or it could mean the murderer was someone who was familiar with dog equipment and competed in conformation. If he or she took the lead with them to her RV . . ."

Red stared at her with admiration. "Then the murder was premeditated."

Chapter 14

We picked apart Red's theories like a dog with a bone until there was no meat left on it.

When no one else had information to share, they turned to me.

"Dr. Morgan, can you have someone check the lead for fingerprints or any other forensic data?"

"I don't think they'll be able to find anything." He glanced around, unsure whether to continue. When he received a slight nod from Red, he continued. "It was very thin and had been pulled tight. I had to cut it out of the folds of her skin. I don't think they'll find fingerprints, but I'll ask."

"Great." I gave him a smile. "Also, maybe they can check if there's anything that might be used to determine where the lead was purchased." I glanced at Dixie. "Are there different types of leads?"

"Oh, yes, this one," she held it up again for us to see, "is wax-coated cotton. It looks and feels like leather. Lots of conformation competitors prefer this brand."

Dr. Morgan promised to take the scraps of the lead that had killed Naomi to the forensics team for analysis, although his face indicated he didn't hold out much hope that they'd find anything useful.

I turned to Stephanie. "I know that you and Mr. Jordan need to focus on Dixie's defense, but I think you both made great progress in finding out information about Warren Keller. I was hoping the two of you . . ."

Theodore Jordan smiled. "I'd love to join forces and see what we can find."

Stephanie smiled and nodded to me.

"Great. I'm hoping you can also check to see if Naomi Keller left a will."

I turned to David. "You're going back to Dixon Vannover's campaign headquarters, right? See if you can find out if there is any gossip about Brittney and Naomi Keller."

I turned to Madison and then gave Red a sideways glance.

Red narrowed his eyes. "What?"

"I'm sure you have Naomi Keller's computer and electronics. I was wondering if Madison could use her, um, *special skills* to check Naomi Keller's e-mails and text messages."

Madison smiled. "I was thinking the same thing." She turned to Red. "Well?"

He nodded.

Monica Jill and B.J. gave me an eager look. "What about us?"

I looked at Monica Jill. "Didn't you say that Dixon Vannover was also into real estate?"

"He's got a finger into a lot of pies, but yes. You want me to ask around and see what I can find out?"

I nodded and then turned to B.J. "I've got two jobs for you. I don't even know if this is possible, but could you check to see if there was an insurance policy on Naomi Keller?"

"I've got friends with all the major insurance companies. If she had a policy, I'll find it." She smiled. "What else do you want me to do?"

"See what you can find out about June Vannover."

"You want me to talk to her?"

"No, actually, I was planning to do that. She seemed to open up to me when she learned that I had gone through a similar situation."

"Well," Dixie said, "I hope you don't think that I'm going to sit back and twiddle my thumbs while you all go out and investigate."

"That goes for me too," Beau said. "I've got a vested interest in finding this killer, and I mean to be in on this investigation from the ground floor."

"I wouldn't expect anything else," I said and smiled at Beau. "David's going to be investigating Dixon Vannover by talking to his campaign volunteers. Monica Jill is going to look at his real estate dealings. I'm hoping you can talk directly to the man himself."

Beau gave me a grin. "I'd love to. Now, what angle do you want me to take?"

"You're a successful businessman. Men like Vannover always need donors. If you were to dangle the idea that you're interested in making a rather large campaign contribution, I think he'd do backflips."

"I can certainly do that."

"What about me?" Dixie asked.

"Brittney Keller seems to have a lot of passion about Greyhounds. I was wondering if you could swing by the Greyhound rescue place and see what you can find out."

"I'd love to. In fact, I would love to help with Greyhound adoption."

"Me too." A man came down the stairs.

We all turned to see who had volunteered to help and were surprised to see Joe Harrison and his Plott Hound, Turbo.

"Joe!" Stephanie rushed over and threw her arms around his neck.

We discreetly looked away to give them a few moments. When they had concluded their greeting, we all took turns welcoming him.

Joe Harrison was tall, dark, and handsome, with piercing blue eyes. He was former military, which is where he had met Red, but now worked in the K-9 division of the Lighthouse Dunes, Indiana, Police Department, along with his faithful four-legged partner, Turbo.

He sat next to Stephanie. "Sorry for crashing the party, but when Stephanie told me about what was happening, I thought I'd come to see if there was anything I could do to help."

Dixie's eyes teared up, and she went over and gave Joe another hug. "Thank you."

"Stephanie can fill you in on the specifics, but . . ." My brain raced, and I had to take several deep breaths to slow it down. "This is perfect."

Red gave me a concerned stare. "I recognize that look."

I ignored him and turned to Dixie. "Didn't you tell me about an organization called Hounds and Heroes?"

Dixie's face beamed. "Oh my God, you're brilliant."

"I wish one of you would fill the rest of us in," B.J. said.

I gave Dixie a nod, indicating she should explain. "Hounds and Heroes is a nonprofit organization that trains retired racing Greyhounds as service dogs for military veterans. Ever since the passage of Amendment Thirteen in Florida, I heard they've been swamped."

B.J. held up a hand. "Wait, what's Amendment Thirteen?"

Dixie took a deep breath to slow herself down. "Amendment Thirteen is a law that bans Greyhound racing in the state of Florida, which was the largest Greyhound racing area in the entire United States, with eleven of the seventeen active dog tracks. Concerned citizens and dog lovers have been trying to get Greyhound racing banned for decades, and now it's finally happened." She sighed. "Fortunately, or unfortunately, that means finding new homes for all those dogs. I've heard there could be as many as eight thousand Greyhounds that were racing in Florida, and over seven thousand were at race-schooling farms."

Red whistled. "That's a lot of dogs. What happens to them now?"

"That's the big question. Greyhound rescue organizations are looking for families to adopt and re-home them. Plus, groups like Hounds and Heroes are training them to help military veterans, but it's slow work, and there are never enough trained volunteers to help."

Joe raised his one hand that wasn't clasped by Stephanie. "Turbo and I would love to help, if we could." He glanced down at Turbo, who was not wearing his vest that indicated he was working, so he was free to roll on the floor with Chyna and Leia.

"Can I help too?" Mai said. "As a former gamekeeper, I certainly have experience with animals, and I spent two years in Her Majesty's Armed Forces." She glanced around. "Plus, I want to help."

"Absolutely, I think all three of you could help," I said, looking from Dixie to Joe to Mai. "It's a worthwhile cause, but there are bound to be different people to question, so see what you can find out."

Dixie nodded. "The dog show world is pretty small. There are bound to be people who knew both Brittney and Naomi."

Before we left, Red cleared his throat. "There's one thing you should all know."

Everyone turned to look at him. I was sitting closest, so I was the only one who saw how tightly his jaw was clenched and the way his scar pulsed.

He took a deep breath. "I was able to stall for a bit, but someone is determined to hang this murder on Dixie."

She gasped and covered her mouth with her hand.

"There's pressure from the top to make a quick arrest." He looked around. "I've got a long track record with the Bureau, and my boss made it clear that was the only reason he was allowing me to drag my feet. Basically, he's given me one week to find the real killer, or they will take me off the case and arrest Dixie."

There was a flash of fear in Dixie's eyes and a cloud of sorrow over Red's, which ignited a flame inside me. I sat up straight. "Then I guess we better get busy finding the real murderer."

Chapter 15

We spent a few minutes fine-tuning our plans, but I wanted to get off the mountain before it was too dark. I said my good-byes to Dixie and Beau, who were both extremely grateful. Then we started the ride swap. I suspected an invisible hand had been involved, but I didn't bother to extract an answer from Red or David. Instead, I agreed to the recommended swaps and made my way outside. Stephanie left with Joe. Madison had ridden to Dixie's house with Red. She must have known that we'd gladly give her a ride home, if needed. Or perhaps she and David had prearranged her ride off the mountain. It didn't much matter to me either way. When Red asked if he could drive me home, which would allow David and Madison to ride together, I didn't argue. As a native of the area, he was adept at mountain driving, and as long as I didn't have to tackle that mountain, I was good.

Our procession down the mountain provided lights, something severely lacking on the mountain at night. Joe and Stephanie were at the front of the line, followed by David and Madison, and Red and I brought up the rear. Theodore Jordan must have lived on the mountain, since he wasn't in the caravan. As a mother, I wanted to know that my children were safely off the mountain, which forced me to keep my eyes open, despite my overwhelming desire to squeeze them shut.

Red must have sensed my concern. "You can close your eyes. I'll let you know when everyone is safe."

I sighed but shook my head. "I can't. I need to know they're all safe." I took a deep breath, gripped the door handle, and forced myself to watch our descent.

"You know, Lookout Mountain isn't really that steep. There are mountains out west that are much taller."

"If that's meant to comfort me, it isn't working." I stole a glance in his direction and then refocused my mental energy on willing our car to stay on the road and not go careening over the side.

He chuckled. "It's actually a really beautiful drive if you would just relax and enjoy it."

"Dennis Olson, I need you to stop talking and focus on the road."

He didn't say another word until we were safely off the mountain and on the highway heading back to my house.

I released my grip on the door and took several deep breaths to steady my nerves and slow down my racing heart. "Are you sure that Stephanie and David—"

"They are both safely off the mountain."

I took a few moments to collect my thoughts before I glanced at him. "I'm sorry."

Even in the dark car, I could tell he was smiling. "It's okay. I know you're not a big fan of our local mountains."

"I know you're used to it, but I don't know if I can ever get used to driving up there."

"If you had the right motivation, I'm sure you'd be able to do it."

I shook my head. "I don't know what that motivation is because I honestly can't see myself ever making that trip."

Once we were on the interstate, it didn't take long to get to my house. I wasn't surprised to find that neither of my kids were there. In fact, I suspected it would be late before either one of them came home.

Inside, I rushed to let Lucky, Aggie, and Rex outside so they could take care of business. When they were done, we sat on the sofa in the living room. Aggie danced around on her hind legs until Red picked her up and petted her. I scooped up Rex, and we scratched and cuddled the poodles. Lucky glanced at the door, as though looking for Stephanie, but eventually lay down on the rug at my feet.

"Did you know Joe was coming tonight?"

"Not until he was in the car and halfway there. He told me he was coming and offered to stay at a hotel, but I assured him my guest room was available."

"This house isn't as big as the rental." I looked around. "Maybe I should look for something a bit larger? I'm scheduled to close at the end of the week. So I could still back out."

He shrugged. "Is that what you want? I thought you loved this house."

"I do love it." I looked at the vaulted ceilings and ugly 1980s architecture that dated the house but also gave it tons of character.

"Then you should buy it. There's plenty of room for you, Aggie, and Rex. It's not like Stephanie and David are moving in."

"No." I released a long sigh. "No matter how much I'd like them to." I leaned my head on Red's shoulder. "I do miss them."

"I never had children, but I'm sure that's natural." He reached one arm around my shoulder, which Aggie wasn't thrilled about.

"You're right. Besides, it's not like I could live close to both of them anyway. Stephanie's in Chicago and David's in New York. I don't suppose that will change anytime soon. Besides, I love Chattanooga. I love the weather and the people. I love being close to Dixie and my new friends like B.J., Monica Jill, Dr. Morgan, Mai, Jacob, and Linda Kay . . . and you." I gave him a poke. "Wow. I have friends."

"Yes, you do."

"No, I have good friends." I twisted so I could face him. "When I met Miss Florrie on that train after meeting with Stephanie and Albert and learning that he not only wanted a divorce, but he wanted to bring his bimb . . . ah, new girlfriend into our home, she got me thinking I needed to find my happy place. When I got home, I remember thinking I had no reason to stay in Lighthouse Dunes. I didn't really have friends . . . not good friends. I didn't like the house, and there was nothing keeping me there."

He leaned over and kissed me. "I am really glad you met Miss Florrie and that you came in search of your happy place." He gazed at me, and I could feel the heat rise up my neck. He leaned over and kissed me again.

After a few minutes or hours, he pulled away. "I better go. Steve Austin won't be happy that he didn't get to come with me."

We took a few additional moments to say good-bye, and then I watched him drive away before I closed the door.

Dating a member of law enforcement had resulted in a couple of very practical gifts, including a home-security system and locks that allowed me to provide my children with entry codes rather than keys. I made sure the doors were locked and the security system engaged before heading off to bed.

I took care of my nightly routine. When I was finished, I had to squeeze into my bed, which was full, with Lucky, Aggie, and Rex already claiming their spots. I wasn't sleepy and lay there thinking about what I'd learned.

Dixon Vannover was a womanizer, and if he was toying with the emotions of Naomi Keller and her daughter, then I could easily see one of them wanting to strangle him. However, would either he or Brittney want to murder Naomi?

Warren Keller was another bad egg. The more I learned about him, the more I could understand why someone might want to murder him, but what would make him want to murder his wife? Could he have found out about her extramarital affairs? He might be a shark when it came to business, but did that make him a murderer?

June Vannover certainly had a reason to want Naomi Keller dead. In fact, perhaps she came to the dog show specifically with murder in mind. But did she follow through with it?

Brittney Keller's syrup protest seemed cruel, but a little syrup was a far cry from murder. Could she have hated her stepmother so much that she'd strangled her?

Ultimately, my mind went back to Naomi Keller. She had managed to infuriate a lot of people in a short period of time at the dog show.

How many other people had she angered?

Chapter 16

Despite my best efforts to sleep, I found myself wide awake late into the night, or rather early into the morning. I refused to admit that my sleeplessness had anything to do with Stephanie and David. The fact that I was able to sleep once I knew they were both home safely was most likely a coincidence.

When my alarm went off, I lay in bed and hoped I could catch another thirty minutes of sleep. Unfortunately, Aggie was having none of it. As soon as the alarm went off, she was wide awake. She stretched out every muscle in her body and then shook herself so hard the entire bed moved. If Rex hadn't already been awake, he certainly was now. Knowing he'd have to go potty now that he was awake, I rolled out of bed and scooped him up quickly and hurried to the back door. When Stephanie came home, she had quietly opened my bedroom door, and Lucky had slipped out around two this morning. So I only had the poodles to worry about.

Normally, I would leave the dogs outside while I took my shower and dressed for work, but today I decided coffee was more important. I put an individual cup into the machine, and within minutes, I could feel the caffeine pumping through my veins. I often wondered who first thought of grinding coffee beans and pouring boiling water over them, but I was eternally grateful.

When Aggie and Rex had finished, I turned to let them in the house, but the door opened, and Lucky bounced out. He made his way down the stairs and found a nice patch of grass near one of the multitude of trees to squat and take care of his business. I glanced around and saw Stephanie come outside with much more energy than I would have thought for a woman who had only had about four hours of sleep. However, she too was drinking the magical elixir of life, so that might have had something to do with it.

She sat and sipped her coffee for several moments before she turned to me. "I can watch them if you want to get ready for work."

I slurped back the last of my coffee and then went inside to shower and dress, which I knew wouldn't take long. The museum wasn't exceptionally formal, and I didn't interact with many of the patrons. However, I generally wore a nice pair of slacks and a blouse rather than a suit, so getting ready didn't take a ton of time. My makeup routine was simple, and today was a day to pull my hair back into a clip rather than fuss. By the time I was dressed and ready for my second cup of coffee, I found David and Stephanie both outside.

"You two are both up early."

David grunted and continued to sip his coffee.

"I'm going to be your chauffeur today," Stephanie said. "If that's okay with you."

"Perfectly fine, but I thought you got a rental?"

"I'm giving it to David." She flushed slightly. "Between Joe and Theodore Jordan, I don't think I'll need it." She turned to face me. "Is that what you're wearing?"

I glanced down at my outfit. "What's wrong with it?"

She paused way too long before responding. "Nothing . . . it's just . . . well, a little . . . casual, don't you think."

"The museum is casual. I won't see anyone today, so no need to get fancy."

She gave me another look that made me ask, "What?"

"Nothing. It's just with your hair like that and . . ." She gestured at my outfit. "You look a bit frumpy."

Frumpy? I tried not to take it personally, but frumpy? I sat for a few moments and then got up and went back inside. This time, I pulled out a skirt and sweater set. I curled my hair and took extra time with my makeup. This time when I walked out, I got a thumbs-up from my daughter and a whistle from my son.

"This just seems like overkill when no one will see me except Linda Kay and Jacob." I sipped my coffee, which was now lukewarm.

"Well, you know you look good," Stephanie said, "and that's the important thing."

I asked Stephanie if she was going to be okay working with Dixie's attorney.

She smiled big. "I just love Mr. Jordan. He is so incredibly nice. Did you know he was involved in the civil rights movement? He actually marched with Dr. Martin Luther King Jr." Her eyes sparkled, and for a brief instant, I saw the little girl I'd raised who was a crusader for justice.

"I didn't know that about him, but I'm not surprised. You know, Beau and Dixie were pretty radical in their day." I took a sip of coffee. "I did my small bit toward fighting for equality too."

My children looked at me with surprise and a tinge of skepticism.

"Really?" David asked.

"Really. Although I wasn't old enough to participate in the civil rights movement, but in college, Dixie and I protested everything from damage to the ozone layer to the university's divestment from companies that supported apartheid." I thought back on my days as a rebel and couldn't help smiling. "I remember walking around with my sign yelling, 'FREE SOUTH AFRICA!' What I don't understand is why you two are so surprised?"

They exchanged glances, but then David said, "I guess you never really think of your mom as some tough militant."

"I was hardly a militant. Although Dixie did get arrested for staging a sit-in in the university president's office." I watched the shock register on their faces. "I had a midterm and was supposed to relieve her afterward, but by the time I got there, the police were dragging them out, and I never took my shift."

David shook his head and then turned to his sister. "Now I know where you get it from."

Stephanie leaned over and kissed me on the cheek. "I love you."

I was happy to know that my children were proud of me, but even happier to know that I could still surprise them. We chatted a little longer, but I still had work to do. So I finished my coffee, and Stephanie shoved her thick hair under an LDPD baseball cap she must have snagged from Joe and then drove me to work.

Stephanie pulled into the lot next to Da Vinci's and parked. "I told David I'd bring back some pastries."

I picked up an apple tart, kissed my daughter, and walked the short distance from the bakery to the museum.

I was surprised to see that Linda Kay was already at her desk when I arrived. "Good morning. You're here awfully early."

She smiled. "I'm glad you're here. I have a meeting with some of the board members. If you're not too busy, maybe you'd like to join us."

"Of course. Is there anything you want me to prepare? I have the financials ready, but—"

"Just bring your wonderful self." She smiled.

Nothing I said could entice Linda Kay to share what this meeting was about. This wasn't the first time she'd asked me to attend a meeting with her, but usually she gave me a heads-up so I could come prepared. She hadn't mentioned wanting to make a large purchase that would require the board's approval. However, I knew she wanted to make some alterations to the older section of the museum, which had been the Hopewell family home. I decided that must be what she wanted me for.

I went to my desk and hurriedly ran a few reports showing that the modest alterations Linda Kay had mentioned to me earlier would bring more visitors to that part of the museum and would pay for itself in two years through increased attendance. When Jacob tapped on my door and told me that Linda Kay was ready, I had what I felt was a stellar presentation prepared.

Even though Linda Kay had a conference table in her office, the board met in a conference room in a secluded area on the main floor.

Jacob knocked on the door, and then we entered.

The regular board meetings were packed with board members and trustees. When everyone was there in full force, there would be over twenty-five people, not including the museum staff who might be invited to present. Today, there were only six people. I recognized them as the board executive committee.

I took a seat at the back of the room and tried to be as quiet and unobtrusive as possible. However, Linda Kay smiled and motioned for me to join her at the main table, so I quickly took my laptop and sat in the seat next to her.

Linda Kay said, "I know you all know Lilly Ann Echosby, who has been filling in as our accountant."

Everyone nodded, and most smiled. Dixon Vannover had his cell phone out and was engrossed in sending a text message, which I thought was extremely rude. However, Linda Kay ignored him and continued. "I don't know what we would have done without Lilly's help these past few months." She smiled at me again, and I forced myself not to squirm in my seat with embarrassment while I plastered a smile on my face.

"I'm pleased to say that Lilly has gotten our books in order, and I received a letter from the IRS that we passed our audit with flying colors."

Everyone applauded, and I felt the heat rise up my neck. I wasn't good at being the center of attention, but I smiled at each board member to acknowledge their gratitude.

"Now that our books are in great shape and we've survived the audit, it's time we made some changes." Linda Kay looked serious. "As you know,

Lilly Ann is a temp, and I think its high time we changed that situation."
She glanced at me and smiled. "So I'm excited to announce that on behalf
of the board, I would like to offer you a full-time, permanent position."

My heart was racing so fast that I wasn't sure I'd actually heard her
correctly. I blinked. "What?"

She laughed. "We're offering you a permanent job." She leaned forward.
"That is, if you're interested."

I flung both my arms around her neck. "Are you serious? Yes. Yes. Of
course."

The other members of the board politely clapped.

I didn't realize I was crying until Jacob handed me a handkerchief.
When I was able to speak, I thanked each member of the board.

"We can discuss the specifics later, but I hoped you would say yes."
Linda Kay nodded, and Jacob opened the door. Stephanie, Joe, David,
Dixie, and Red came in. Dixie was carrying a cake.

I hugged Stephanie. "Thank you."

"For what?"

"Goading me about the way I looked so I'd change clothes and put on
makeup."

Stephanie hugged me. "Jacob called and invited us, and I thought you
might want to look your best."

I squeezed her. I wasn't a vain woman, but she knew I'd want to make
sure I looked my best, especially if I was going to be the center of attention.

Red and David both brought flowers, which made me start crying all
over again.

Jacob clapped and yelled, "*Speech!*"

I have no idea what I said. I remember thanking Linda Kay, Jacob, and
the board, and then I think I babbled on for several moments before I finally
realized I was making a complete fool of myself and stopped talking.

Jacob wheeled in a cart with paper plates, plastic silverware, and plastic
fluted glasses. That's when I noticed that Stephanie and Joe had brought
a few bottles of champagne. While Dixie cut the cake, Jacob poured the
champagne, and Stephanie distributed it around. When everyone had a
glass, Dixon Vannover stood up and proposed a toast and wished me many
happy years at the museum.

I introduced my family to the various board members and tried to stop
getting weepy whenever anyone congratulated or welcomed me to the
Hopewell Museum family, but it was a losing battle. I was an emotional
basket case.

The cake was chocolate with chocolate icing. It looked handmade and was extremely moist. I found myself licking my fork and didn't even realize my eyes were closed until I opened them and saw Red looking at me with a grin on his face. "What?"

He shook his head. "Nothing. I was just wondering if you needed a few moments alone with that cake. You seemed to be enjoying it so much."

I put my fork down and stuck out my tongue before I remembered where I was. I quickly glanced around to make sure none of the board members had seen my childish behavior. I was glad to find everyone was engrossed in enjoying their own cake and champagne. I turned to Dixie, who was sitting next to me. "This cake is delicious. It doesn't taste store-bought. Did Mrs. Huntington bake this?"

"No, but please don't tell her that I allowed anyone other than her to bake for you. She'd be devastated. Actually, I ordered this from a friend of mine. Melinda makes the best chocolate cake I've ever had."

"It's delicious." I glanced down at my plate, which I'd all but licked clean. "Does she have a shop, or does she cater? Maybe I could order a couple of cakes for the housewarming."

Dixie smiled. "She doesn't have a shop, but I'm sure she'd make whatever you want. She's amazing."

Dixie and I talked about the menu for the housewarming, which had been all but forgotten because of the murder investigation. We decided on a chocolate cake, two dozen cupcakes, and something Dixie called whoopie pies. She promised to place the order with Melinda, and I turned my attention to Red. He was chatting with Joe but kept glancing in Dixon Vannover's direction.

"Stop staring," I whispered.

"I'm not staring."

I glanced down at the end of the table where Dixon Vannover was sitting and sipping champagne. There was a plate with a generous slice of chocolate cake sitting in front of him, but he hadn't touched it. Instead, he had his cell phone out and was texting while pretending to listen to Linda Kay, who was next to him. I grabbed Red's arm. "Come on."

We walked down to the end of the table.

"Excuse me, Mr. Vannover."

"Yes?" He continued to text, but I waited until he stopped and looked up.

"I wanted to say thank you for making me a permanent member of the staff here at the museum. Linda Kay is wonderful, and I'm sure I'll learn so much working for her."

He grinned and mumbled something and then returned to his phone.

"I'd like to introduce you to my boyfriend, Dennis Olson." He nodded without looking away from his phone.

"He's with the Tennessee Bureau of Investigation, and he's investigating the murder of Naomi Keller."

That got his attention. The arrogant jerk finally looked at Red, and fear flashed across his face.

"Red, this is Dixon Vannover."

The two men shook hands.

"I know Red has been anxious to talk to you, so I thought there's no time like the present."

Dixon Vannover's phone vibrated, but miracle of miracles, he completely ignored it. Instead, the color that I'd seen rising up his neck flooded his face. He looked like a blotchy tomato. "You want to talk to me? I can't imagine why."

"Your name came up during the course of our murder investigation. Do you mind if I sit down?"

"Of course not." He pointed to the empty seat next to him. "Please."

I gave Linda Kay a sideways glance. She looked like a cat who'd just eaten a large bowl of cream. She winked at me and turned her attention to her cake.

Red sat down. "How well did you know Naomi Keller?"

Dixon Vannover squirmed, and I could almost see the wheels turning in his eyes. He glanced around like a rabbit caught in a trap. "I knew her, of course, but no better than anyone else."

Red gave him his deadpan law-enforcement face that gave nothing away. "My sources indicate that you and Naomi Keller were rather close. In fact, I hear you're also close to her daughter Brittney."

I hadn't thought Dixon Vannover's face could get redder than it was before, but he was now turning purple, his tomato face turning into eggplant. He scowled at Linda Kay, who gave a look of pure innocence. "Those are malicious lies. It's fake news planted by my political opponents to try and ruin my good name and place a black mark against my character. I don't have to sit here and be insulted by some . . . some . . . vigilante TBI officer." He stood and grabbed his phone. "You have no right to disparage my good name by questioning me here."

Red stood too. "Actually, you're right. You don't have to sit here. We can go downtown." He pulled out his shield and held it up. "However, this badge gives me the right to question you. I just thought you would prefer to do it here in a friendly setting. However, if you'd rather go to headquarters, that's fine too."

Dixon Vannover's face went from outrage to despair in less than ten seconds. He glanced around the room. Then he leaned close and whispered, "Can we go someplace a little more private?"

"Lead the way."

Dixon Vannover flashed a toothy grin at the other board members. Obviously, he was under the false impression that no one had witnessed his humiliating exhibition. However, if he was entertaining that thought, he was sorely wrong.

He picked up his glass of champagne, and only those closest to him saw how his hand shook. He drained the liquid and replaced the glass. He extended a hand to me. "Welcome aboard." We shook. Then he waved to the group. "I'm sorry to leave such an exciting party, but I have a little business to take care of." He chuckled. "No rest for the wicked." He slapped a hand on Red's back, as though they were old buddies heading out for a beer, and walked out.

Red turned and beckoned for Joe to join him.

"That was amazing," Linda Kay said. "I just love Red. I sure hope you marry that man."

I felt flushed. "Let's not get ahead of ourselves and count a proposal before it's offered."

I had to work really hard to keep from smiling.

Chapter 17

The party ended not long after Red, Joe, and Dixon Vannover left. The board members welcomed me and then hurried on to other meetings. I noticed Dixie and Jacob cleaning up, and I hurried over to lend a hand.

Jacob waved me away. "There's not much to do. Besides, you're the guest of honor. You aren't supposed to soil your hands with this trivial nonsense."

"Pshaw. We're a team."

"There's not much cleanup." He grinned. "It hurt my heart to use disposable plates and plastic silverware, but . . . it sure makes life easy."

Every piece of cake was gone. Dixie tossed the box into the trash. All of the champagne was gone too, and the empty bottles were also tossed. The plates, silverware, and napkins were chucked into the trash.

Jacob picked up the two bouquets of flowers. "Do you want me to put these in your office, or do you want to take them home?"

I thought for a moment. "My office."

He put them on his cart. "Then I better get them in water." Before leaving, he turned to Linda Kay. "You have another meeting in ten minutes." Then he pushed the cart out of the room.

Linda Kay motored her scooter toward the door, and David jumped up to hold it open for her. She gave him a big smile. "I've got to scoot." She waved and rolled a few feet before stopping and turning toward me. "Why don't you take the afternoon off and enjoy your family. Tomorrow, we can talk about the specifics."

I thanked her, and she rolled away.

I looked at Dixie, Stephanie, and David. "Thank you all for coming, but what do we do now?"

"How about we grab some lunch and figure it out," Dixie said.

"I need to go upstairs to my office and get my purse." I picked up my laptop. "And I need to take this back. I'll be down in a few minutes, and we can go."

I rushed upstairs. Jacob was quick. Both sets of flowers had been placed in beautiful crystal vases and were sitting on my desk. I stopped to sniff each and knew that I had a silly grin on my face, but I didn't really care. I had a permanent job at a place I liked and got to work with people I liked. I snatched my purse from my desk drawer. Jacob wasn't at his desk, and Linda Kay's door was closed. So I hurried downstairs.

Dixie and Stephanie were waiting for me in Dixie's Lexus. I climbed into the passenger seat and buckled up.

She pulled out of the parking lot, and that's when I noticed David pull behind her. I turned to my friend. "Where are we going?"

"Stephanie sent a text to Joe letting the boys know we were going to Aretha Frankensteins." She glanced in my direction. "You can't spend time in Chattanooga without going there." She made a quick right turn in front of a city bus and headed down an extremely narrow street with more speed than I would have deemed wise. However, Dixie never seemed to attract the attention of the police, no matter how fast she drove.

When my stomach traveled back down from my mouth, I opened my eyes and released my grip on the door. "I don't think I've ever been to Aretha Frankensteins."

"That's on me. I have been derelict in my duties as an ambassador for Chattanooga." She turned down what appeared to be a quiet residential street. After about two blocks, she slowed down. "There's a spot." She swerved and pulled into a parking space almost directly in front of a large house. The parking gods were almost always looking out for Dixie. Unfortunately, David wasn't as lucky, and he had to circle the block.

We climbed the stone steps and walked up to the covered, wraparound porch. A creative builder had fitted a bar around the railing, and there were people sitting on barstools. Inside, the restaurant was packed; and a large bar dominated the main room, and the tables around the perimeter offered barely enough room to walk between them. The sloped ceilings and every available wall were decorated with pictures. The combination of the small interior jam-packed with people, the cluttered walls, and the noise sent me into sensory overload.

A petite woman who was extremely pregnant greeted us. "How many?"

"Six," Dixie said. "Any tables outside?"

The hostess waddled to a side door and looked outside. Then she motioned for us to follow her.

Outside, the wraparound porch bar was crowded, and from the side I could see, there was another level with tables that were placed on a concrete pad, with a large umbrella to protect diners from the sun.

She pulled two plastic chairs from a nearby table and then left, promising that our server would soon arrive with water.

We sat and stared at the menu, which had a Halloween theme.

David smiled. "I don't think I've ever been to a restaurant where they advertise that it may take quite a while to get your food."

"What?" I asked.

David read, "Everything is prepared to order in our tiny kitchen. Please understand, waiting thirty minutes or more for your food is not uncommon. That said, thank you for coming, and enjoy." He looked over the top of his menu and smiled. "I love the South."

"This place is famous," Dixie said. "I believe it was once featured on Rachael Ray's show—you know, the one where she traveled and had to eat under some ridiculous amount, like forty dollars."

Stephanie smiled. "Oh, I used to like that show."

"So she came to Chattanooga and ate at Aretha Frankensteins."

"It's very . . . eclectic?" David said.

He looked up and waved. We all turned to see who he was waving at and caught sight of Joe and Red coming around the corner. Without even thinking about it, we automatically adjusted and skootched our seats so Red could sit next to me and Joe next to Stephanie.

"Did he confess to the murder?" Dixie asked.

"Unfortunately, he didn't confess to anything." Red glanced up at the waitress, who arrived and took our beverage orders. When she was gone, we turned back to Red and he continued. "He wouldn't even admit to his name being Dixon Vannover. He spent the majority of the time whining about how his political opponents were trying to cast black marks against his character and *besmirch* his name."

"Besmirch?" I said. "He actually used that word?"

"He did."

"I don't think I've ever heard anyone actually say *besmirch*," Joe said, laughing.

"I'm surprised Dixon Vannover knows what the word means," Dixie said. "Beau claims he's dumber than a bag of hammers."

Stephanie had chosen that instant to take a sip of her coffee and nearly choked laughing. "I don't think I've ever heard that saying before."

The waitress hovered near our table, and we knew it was time to get down to business.

David asked, "What do you recommend?"

The young woman mentioned the restaurant was famous for its pancakes and waffles. She recommended the Waffle of Insane Greatness. David took her up on her recommendation. Dixie mentioned that was her favorite and ordered the same thing. Red surprised me by ordering the Slim Stack, which was two pancakes. I'd seen him eat and knew he was capable of putting back a lot more than two pancakes. I was feeling super hungry and ordered the Fat Stack, which was three pancakes. Red and Dixie gave me a look.

"What?"

"Their pancakes are large," Red said. "Are you sure you're up for that?"

"Is that a challenge?"

Red held up his hands, and he and Dixie exchanged a glance.

Stephanie ordered something called Elephants Gerald, which I'd noticed on the menu because it involved a Belgian waffle topped with vanilla ice cream, pecans, syrup, and cinnamon.

Once our orders were placed, the waitress took our menus and headed back to put in our orders.

"So Dixon Vannover refused to answer questions?" I asked, surprised that Red would allow him to get away with that.

"No, he answered. He just lied. He denied having a relationship with Naomi Keller. He denied having ever been in a relationship with Brittney Keller."

Joe grinned. "At one point, he denied being in a relationship with anyone, but he must have realized how that sounded, and he backtracked and said he was married and hadn't been involved in any relationships outside of his marriage."

"There are plenty of people who know that isn't true," Dixie said. "He has to realize you'll figure out the truth."

Joe shrugged.

"But didn't you tell him that his wife actually showed up at the dog show and confronted Naomi Keller in front of you?" I stared at Red. "She told us that he was having an affair with Naomi Keller and that he planned to get divorced."

"When I told him that, he blanched and said that I must have been confused."

"You have got to be joking."

"When he realized that he couldn't convince me I was wrong, he said his wife must have been confused."

"He completely threw his wife under the bus," Joe added.

"He claimed she was 'high-strung' and jealous and often got confused." Red barely had the words out of his mouth before Dixie, Stephanie, and I were ready to pounce.

"High-strung!"

"Don't shoot the messengers. We're just reporting what the man said."

"Why that slimy, bald-faced liar." Dixie folded her arms across her chest and scowled. "I wish I had been there. I'd have grabbed that little weasel by the short hairs and helped him understand what *high-strung* really means."

We glanced at Dixie until she looked up and smiled. "Sorry, but that just burns my biscuits when someone accuses a woman of being *high-strung* simply because she is passionate."

"Or, in this case, honest," Stephanie said. "It's insulting and belittling and—"

David held up a hand. "We get it. Dixon Vannover is a liar, but they're just relaying what happened."

I took a deep breath and turned to Red. "David's right. What else did he say?"

"That's pretty much it. He denied having 'carnal knowledge' of both Naomi Keller and Brittney Keller." He used air quotes to indicate the choice of words belonged to Dixon Vannover. "He also threatened to sue me, the Tennessee Bureau of Investigation, and anyone who accused him of infidelity if this 'pack of lies' made its way into the newspapers."

"I'd love to see him try," Stephanie said. "I'd wipe the floor with him."

Our waitress and two others, all laden with plates, made their way to our table. When the waitress placed Red's plate in front of him, I knew I was in trouble. His two pancakes covered the entire surface of the plate and were each at least an inch tall.

When the mountain of pancakes was placed in front of me, I was blown away by their size. There was no way I would be able to make the slightest dent in those. I glanced at Red, who smiled. "I tried to warn you."

"Oh, shut up."

He chuckled and then switched his plate with mine. He gave me a look that asked, *Is that better?* I nodded and mouthed, *Thank you.*

Everything looked and smelled delicious. We took a break from our recaps to dig into our food.

I wasn't able to finish even one of the two pancakes on my plate. Red fared better and managed to eat about half of the three pancakes. No one managed to eat everything, although Joe came the closest and finished three-quarters of his Belgian waffle.

When the waitress came back to check on us and to find out how we wanted our bills distributed, Dixie handed her a credit card and told her she was paying the entire bill. I was accustomed to Dixie's generosity, but Red and Joe put up a bit of an argument.

Dixie waved away all protests. "I'm paying for this, and I don't want any arguments. You're all here because of me." She glanced at David, Joe, and Stephanie and choked up. "If I wasn't under suspicion, Red would have turned this case over to the Chattanooga Police or allowed that troll to arrest whoever he wanted." She took her napkin and dabbed at her eyes. "Please, let me do this."

I reached over and gave her arm a squeeze.

She pulled herself together and took a deep breath. "Besides, if you hadn't noticed, we like to feed people in the South."

We chuckled. When Dixie had signed her bill, I asked, "What now?"

Red glanced at his watch. "I've got to get back to work. I need to find out if I'm going to need to issue a warrant to get Dixon Vannover back or if his attorney wants him to voluntarily come in to make a statement."

Stephanie was going to meet Theodore Jordan at the courthouse. Joe and Dixie had plans to go to the Greyhound rescue. I wanted to go home and change clothes. David said he was headed to Vannover campaign headquarters, which was only a block away from the Vannovers' house. He offered to take me home so I could change, and then he'd drop me off to talk to June. That meant Dixie wouldn't have to go out of her way. We made our way to our respective vehicles and set out to tackle our suspects. Normally, Dixie would be teaching obedience on Tuesday nights, but at last night's meeting, we agreed to forego the class and meet for pizza at my house.

David offered to bring the car up to get me, but I needed the exercise and decided to accompany him. It was a beautiful, sunny day, and I enjoyed looking at the older homes in this neighborhood.

It didn't take long to get home. David let Aggie, Rex, and Lucky out while I changed, which didn't take long at all. Aggie wasn't thrilled about the fact that we were leaving again so quickly, but when I pulled out my secret weapon, string cheese, she was attentive. I was amazed at the power a stick of string cheese had on such a little dog. One minute, she was chasing Rex around the house, but now she was sitting by my side, waiting for her cheese. I took the time to cut the cheese into small pieces. Rex and Aggie were small, so the two of them shared half a piece of cheese. Lucky was much bigger, but I didn't want him to be bound up later, so I cut only a half piece of cheese for him too.

When I was done, Aggie and Rex raced to the bedroom and were standing in their crate, ready for their treat. After I finished, David drove to the Vannover campaign.

Dixon Vannover had rented a small retail store in a strip mall for his campaign headquarters. David turned down a side street to a gated community. Dixie had given me the address last night, so when David pulled up to the gate, he punched in the house numbers, which rang the Vannover intercom.

I recognized June Vannover's voice. "Mrs. Vannover, it's Lilly Echosby. We met at the dog show over the weekend. I wanted to check on you and make sure you're okay."

"Yes, I remember you. That's so nice of you." She quickly gave me directions to her house and then buzzed the gate, which opened to admit us.

David followed her directions and pulled up to a large, Georgian brick home that looked big enough to house a small army. We pulled up the circular driveway.

David gazed up at the McMansion and whistled. "You could fit my entire New York brownstone inside and still have room left over."

The house was huge. It was a new brick house that was meant to look like an older New England Georgian that had been added onto over the years.

"It's certainly massive."

"Do they have a large family?" David asked.

"It's just the two of them. I suppose they entertain a lot." I sat and stared at the house. A shiver went down my spine.

"Do you want me to go in with you?" My son looked concerned.

"I'll be fine. You go to the campaign headquarters and see what you can find." I got out of the car, closed the door, and marched toward the front door.

I wasn't intimidated by the size of the house or the gated community. Dixie didn't live in a gated community, but her house was most likely bigger and more expensive. Yet I couldn't deny there was something that made me uneasy.

By the time I got to the front door, it was opened by an older woman I assumed was the housekeeper. She smiled. "Mrs. Vannover is expecting you."

I stepped into the two-story entry, which had a curved staircase leading to the second floor, hardwood floors, and a wingback chair that looked as though it had never been sat in. The housekeeper led me past a formal living room to a family room at the back of the house. The room was decorated in a monochromatic color scheme with light, almost white, carpet, walls, and furniture. The sofa where June Vannover sat was a rich dark espresso leather that looked worn but comfortable. Despite the cool color palette, the room felt warm and inviting, whether due to the bright pops of color that were placed around the room, including the bright red swag set atop the floor-to-ceiling windows, the bright pillows, and the large fireplace that June Vannover had lit despite the warm day.

"Lilly, what an . . . unexpected surprise."

Her face, body language, and tone indicated that my *unexpected* visit wasn't necessarily a welcome one. Nevertheless, I put a fake smile on my face and thought about Dixie. This was for Dixie. After a few moments of awkward smiles and silence, June caved into good manners and asked me to sit.

She was stretched out on the sofa and didn't get up, so my seating options were limited. I chose an oversized chair placed near the opposite end of the sofa where she was sitting and perched on the edge.

Now that I was seated, my own good manners required me to start the conversation. "I was worried about you and wanted to make sure you were okay."

"Worried? Why on earth would you worry about me?" She flashed a smile that said, *Now that my rival for my husband's affections is dead, there's no need to worry about me.*

"You were so distressed Saturday when we talked."

She gazed at me as though she had no recollection of who I was, what I was talking about, or what day of the week it was. June Vannover was a better actress than I gave her credit for because I was almost sure she couldn't be as clueless as her face indicated.

The housekeeper who had shown me inside returned with a tea tray, which she placed on the coffee table near Mrs. Vannover. June swung her legs down and poured. "I love a good cup of tea. Would you care for one?"

I honestly didn't want tea, but refusing would only end my visit sooner than I wanted. "I'd love some."

She handed me the filled cup and poured herself another. We sat sipping tea for a few moments in silence, June Vannover probably thinking she'd successfully convinced me that she was indeed fine, without a care in the world, and me wondering how I could shock her into telling me that her husband had murdered Naomi Keller.

I placed my teacup on a coaster. "June, I'm going to assume by your attitude that now that Naomi Keller is dead, your husband has decided to stay and you feel your marriage is safe, but I can assure you—"

June Vannover leapt to her feet. "I . . . I can't believe . . . you have no right."

"You're right. I have no right to come into your home and poke holes into the fake bubble of lies that you've chosen to surround yourself with."

"I don't know what you're talking about."

"You're denying that your husband cheated."

"Dixon is a wonderful man. He would never do anything so despicable and low." She leaned forward and pointed her finger. "Just because you weren't able to keep your own husband satisfied doesn't mean that other women are in the same boat." She glared down at me. "I won't stand by while you make slanderous statements about Dixon intended to ruin his good name and political career."

I felt the heat rise up my neck, but not because I cared about Albert. I was well over my late husband. If he hadn't cheated and left me, I would have been stuck in a loveless marriage, and I might never have found happiness in Tennessee with Red. No, I was angry at the smug look on her face when she, of all people, had no right to it. "Don't you think you should have thought about this before you drove to the dog show, where you were seen and heard screaming at Naomi Keller in front of a crowd of people, including a TBI officer?"

She blanched.

"You told me, in front of witnesses, that your husband was leaving you for Naomi Keller because she was pregnant with his child. Did you know that she wasn't?"

If I thought her face was pale before, that was nothing to the way it looked now. She went completely white.

"Wasn't what?" she whispered.

"Pregnant."

She flopped down onto the sofa and stared up at me. "Are you sure?"

"According to the autopsy, she not only wasn't pregnant, but she'd had a hysterectomy. So she couldn't have children."

June Vannover burst into tears. I sat down next to her and comforted her the best I could. After a few moments, she looked up. "You don't know . . . what this means. I was so afraid, because of the baby . . . Dixon wanted children but . . . I wanted to adopt, but he didn't want to raise someone else's children. The doctors said it was Dixon, but then when Naomi Keller got pregnant, he said it couldn't have been him." She sobbed. "We had a horrible fight, and then I followed him to the dog show and—"

Chapter 18

As soon as the words were spoken, she knew she'd blown it and slapped her hand over her mouth. Her eyes were wide and frightened. When she was able to speak, she mumbled, "He's right. I'm a dumb, stupid, idiot who is going to ruin his political career."

I pulled her hands off her mouth and stared into her eyes. "You are not. You're not dumb or stupid, and you're not an idiot. You're not the one who cheated. You're not the one who risked ruining a political career by having an adulterous affair. Your only fault is that you love someone who doesn't respect you."

She stared at me for several moments and then burst into tears.

The housekeeper came back to see what the ruckus was about.

"Mrs. Vannover has had a bit of a shock. Do you have some brandy?"

She nodded and hurried out of the room. She was back quickly with a tray bearing a crystal decanter and two glasses. She placed them on the coffee table next to the tea tray and hurried out.

I poured some of the amber liquid into the tea and handed it to my hostess.

She gulped it down so quickly I knew this wasn't her first exposure to spirits. When she finished her brandy-laced tea, she refilled her cup with just the brandy and tossed it back.

I knew she wasn't ready to hear this truth, but I had to at least try. "You need to tell the police he was there." She started to shake her head before I finished talking. "You have to tell the truth."

"I can't. He's my husband." She held a pillow to her chest. "He said I wouldn't have to. A wife doesn't have to testify against her husband."

"That's only true when it comes to court. He hasn't been charged with anything. I'm not asking you to testify against him. I'm only asking you to tell the police the truth, that he was at the dog show." She looked leery. "If he's innocent, then he has nothing to worry about."

After a few moments, she glanced at me. "Do you have a job?" She hurried to add, "Outside the home?"

I smiled. "I'm a certified public accountant, a CPA. I work at the Hopewell Museum."

"You have a career. You know how to do things—support yourself. The only thing I've ever been trained to is to be a wife and mother." She dropped her gaze. "And I couldn't even do that right."

It took all of the inner strength I could muster not to grab her shoulders and try to shake some sense into her. Instead, I took a deep breath and chose to shock her out of self-doubt. "If you were tested and your doctor said there's no reason you can't have children, then it would seem logical that Dixon is the problem, not you."

"But he said . . . I mean, he's so virile . . . and . . ."

"That has nothing to do with it." I hoped to get away from talking about Dixon Vannover's manhood by focusing the conversation in a different direction. I glanced around the room. "You've created a lovely home. This room is beautiful. I absolutely love the artwork and pops of color."

She beamed. "Those are mine."

"You're joking. You painted those?"

"I love art." She got up and walked to the paintings. "These are acrylics, but I've been dabbling in watercolors lately." She picked up a brightly painted vase. "I took a pottery class, which was a lot of fun." She returned the pot and shrugged. "Dixon didn't like it. He said art has to be bought from an art dealer."

"Dixon is wrong. You're talented. I'm not an expert, but since I started working at the museum, I have learned that art doesn't have to be expensive."

She smiled. "Would you like to see more?"

"Absolutely."

She took me on a tour of the house. Most of the rooms were meticulously decorated and looked as though they belonged in a designer showroom. The living room was picture-perfect, but cold. However, June had always found a way to provide one touch of her own by adding a small pot or miniature picture, giving the rooms life. When we'd finished the grand tour of the six-bedroom, five-bathroom house, she took me outside to her artist's shed.

"Dixon and I fought over the shed. He said it would look like a hillbilly outhouse." She smiled. "However, when the neighbors all started getting man caves or she-sheds, then he gave in."

The exterior of the artist's shed matched the house, which I guessed was Dixon's requirement. Inside, the room was a true artist's studio, with paint, clay, and a pottery wheel and kiln. One side of the shed was all glass sliding doors, providing light and allowing nature into the room. The remaining walls were covered with brightly colored canvases that reminded me of the Caribbean. A large orange cat was curled up on a bench, where a ray of sunlight shone into the room. The cat opened an eye as we entered but must have deemed us unworthy of further consideration and went back to sleep.

June walked over and picked up the cat. "This is Rembrandt."

I walked over and tentatively extended a hand to pet him. The cat barely glanced at me. I stroked his fur and was rewarded by a deep purr.

"He just showed up about a year ago." June cradled the cat like a baby. "I have to keep him out here because Dixon is allergic, but that's fine with me. He's good company." She snuggled the cat close and whispered gibberish about how good and beautiful he was.

I glanced around the studio and was quickly intrigued by a painting of a leaf.

"This is amazing. Have you sold any of your paintings?"

June shook her head. "Who would pay money for these?"

I stared at her. "I would." I held up the leaf painting. "Would you consider selling this one?"

She stared. "You really want it?"

"Yes. It would look great over my fireplace. How much?"

She shook her head. "I couldn't sell that. You can have it."

I wanted to take the painting and run, but my conscious wouldn't let me. "I can't take it. This picture is really good."

"Fifty dollars?" she said shyly.

I shook my head. "That's ridiculous."

She hung her head.

"How about two hundred?"

She gasped. "Dollars? Are you serious?"

"I'm sure you can get a lot more, but since neither of us are experts, let's start there."

She gave me a curious look. "I can't believe you want to pay me two hundred dollars for one of my paintings. You're not just trying to make me feel better. I mean, you really think it's worth two hundred dollars?"

"I can't afford to pay two hundred dollars to make someone feel better. Honestly, I think it's worth more than two hundred dollars, but since I'm your first sale, I'm willing to consider this a perk for discovering a new artist. Would you be okay if I took some pictures to show one of my friends at the art museum?"

She agreed, so I pulled out my cell phone and took pictures. I sent the pictures to Linda Kay. When I was done, I turned to her. "Will you take a check?"

We went back inside and took care of business.

She stared at the check. "I can't believe someone paid money for one of my paintings. You aren't just doing this so I'll tell the police that Dixon was at the dog show? Because I won't—"

I held up a hand. "Whether you decide to tell the truth or not has nothing to do with my buying your painting. I genuinely love it. The rest is between you and your conscience." With that parting remark, I said my good-byes and left.

The subdivision was a short distance from the campaign headquarters, but the walk was awkward, especially as I had a large canvas in tow. However, I made it and found my car with no trouble. It took a little rearranging to get the canvas into the back, but I was determined. When I finished, instead of going inside and risking a run-in with Dixon Vannover, I waited in the car, which was great for sitting and enjoying the day and thinking.

While I waited, Linda Kay replied to my text messages with a text full of capital letters and exclamation marks. She wanted to know who the artist was and how she could get her hands on those paintings. Praise from Linda Kay put a smile on my face. She had a ton of questions, and it didn't take long for me to realize that I had very few answers. After a great deal of back and forth, we realized the best plan was to skip the middleman. She said she would reach out to June Vannover directly. I sat and enjoyed the sunshine and hoped that June Vannover would realize that she was talented and deserved more than being treated like Dixon Vannover's doormat.

Lost in thought, I nearly leapt out of my skin when I heard a knock. When my pulse stopped racing, I rolled down my window. "Jacob, you nearly gave me a heart attack."

"Sorry, but I recognized your car and thought I'd say hello."

"What are you doing here?"

"Linda Kay was so excited about the paintings you sent her that she wanted me to get here right away."

"She really thinks they're good? She's not just humoring me?"

"Linda Kay Weyman is a nice lady, but she doesn't play around where art is concerned."

I released a breath. "Thank goodness. June Vannover couldn't take rejection. She's . . . fragile."

"I don't think she'll need to be concerned about rejection."

Jacob's phone dinged after a few minutes. When the dings became faster, he glanced at the incoming text messages and said, "I'd better get a move on or Linda Kay is going to skin me alive."

We said our good-byes, and I hoped that Jacob would love June's art as much as I did. I was tempted to walk back to the Vannovers' house but resisted the temptation. My emotions were fickle. In no time flat, I had moved from excitement for June Vannover to concern for her well-being. What if Dixon Vannover rebelled against his wife's success? I didn't see any visible indications of physical abuse, although the verbal and emotional abuse was bad enough.

While I pondered my next move, Dixie sent a text letting me know that she was going to drop off a casserole at Warren Keller's house and wanted to know if I was interested in joining her. Not sure how much longer David would be, I agreed. She was just five minutes away, so I didn't have long to wait.

Dixie pulled up beside me, and I transferred my painting to her car before getting in myself. Dixie's response was better than I could have hoped.

"I can't believe you got that for two hundred dollars."

"Do you think I should have offered her more? I don't want to take advantage of her."

Dixie pulled out onto Gunbarrel Road. "You offered her four times what she asked. You got a great deal. Honestly, she probably would have given you the painting for free."

We chatted about art, and Dixie took the familiar path toward her house. When she started her ascent of Lookout Mountain, I closed my eyes and braced myself.

"You didn't tell me Warren Keller lived up Lookout Mountain."

Dixie laughed. "Would you have come if I did?"

"No."

She chuckled. "Now you know why I didn't tell you."

When we reached the top, I could feel the car level out and knew it was safe to open my eyes.

Dixie pulled up to a large, sprawling, brick-and-stone estate. Unlike Dixon Vannover's home, which was a new house meant to look old, Warren Keller's home was an older one that had been meticulously updated to look modern.

"That's impressive."

Dixie reached into the back seat and pulled out a glass casserole dish. "I've heard the inside is even more impressive."

We walked up the winding cobblestone path to the front door and rang the bell. We were both slightly surprised that Warren Keller opened the door himself instead of a maid. However, he seemed equally surprised to see us.

"Dixie, I didn't expect to see you."

"Naomi and I weren't close, but Beau and I still wanted to express our condolences on your loss." She held up her casserole.

After a brief hesitation, he widened the door. "Forgive my manners. Please come in."

"We don't want to intrude on your grief, so if you'll just direct me to the kitchen, I'll put this in the fridge and be on my way."

"Of course, follow me." He led the way to the kitchen.

Along the way, I noted the newer windows, elegant furnishings, and thick carpets. I gazed outside and noticed that a large cat had made itself comfortable and was sunning near the back window. The kitchen had old-world charm, but it had clearly been modernized. Marble counters, a super-sized commercial fridge, and red knobs on a massive gas cooktop told me no expense had been spared on this elegantly simple room.

When Warren opened the fridge, it was clear that Dixie's wasn't the first casserole he'd received. He chuckled. "Looks like I'm going to be eating casseroles for quite some time."

"I guess it's just a Southern thing. If someone dies, you bring a casserole. If you'd rather not—"

"Don't you dare take that dish." He reached out and held it close to his chest. "I intend to have a casserole smorgasbord. Would you and your friend care for coffee?"

"Forgive my manners. This is my friend, Lilly Ann Echosby. Lilly Ann, this is Warren Keller."

We shook hands, and I mumbled condolences.

The Kellers had a fancy coffee machine that was capable of single servings or a pot. Warren seemed adept at maneuvering the massive beast, and before long, it sputtered, steamed, and spewed a dark liquid that smelled heavenly.

When the pot was ready, he placed it on a tray, and we followed him into a family room that looked out onto a secluded, green, lush backyard.

Coffees distributed, we sat back and sipped in an uncomfortable silence. Eventually, I said, "You have a beautiful home."

"Thank you. We'd just finished the last of the renovations." He choked up, but quickly recovered. "Naomi wasn't a big fan. She preferred modern design, and would have preferred we sell and move into one of those metal and glass box condos downtown, but we needed the space for the dogs."

It wasn't until he mentioned the dogs that I realized what was missing. I hadn't seen any dogs or dog accessories. Every dog owner I knew had dogs, dog toys, or treats everywhere. Even Dixie's immaculate home had the occasional dog toy. "Where are your dogs?"

"Oh, they aren't here. My daughter, Brittney, took them. She is going to try to re-home them."

I was so surprised I didn't know how to respond, so I didn't say anything.

"How are you holding up?" Dixie asked. "Do you need anything?"

Warren put his coffee down. "I don't really know. I don't suppose it's really sunk in yet. I'm hoping that when the police have arrested her murderer, I'll have some peace." There was a long, uncomfortable silence. "I don't suppose you've heard something? The police don't really tell me anything." He glanced from Dixie to me and then added, "I'd heard that you are friendly with the officer in charge."

I glanced at Dixie for help. She put down her coffee cup. "I don't believe the police have arrested anyone."

"Excuse me, but I had heard that they were looking at you." He hurriedly added, "Absolutely absurd, of course. I told that policeman that I knew you and Naomi didn't get along, but there was no way that you'd resort to murder."

"Thank you." Dixie patted his arm. "I don't know that I'm completely off the hook yet, but there are several others that have a much better reason for murder than me."

He sat up. "Who?"

Dixie and I exchanged a glance. I gave a shrug, and she continued. "Well, this is just my own opinion, but, well, Dixon Vannover."

Warren Keller looked surprised. "Do you know why?"

This time the looks Dixie and I exchanged were intercepted. Warren Keller inserted himself. "Please, I don't think you could tell me anything that I haven't already heard, but it's killing me not knowing."

"Well, we had heard that there might have been something going on between Dixon Vannover and Naomi . . . and possibly Brittney." We gazed intently for a reaction.

Warren Keller hung his head. "Well, I suspected there might have been someone else, but . . . Dixon Vannover? Are you sure?"

"Of course not, but you were at the dog show when she showed up."

Warren Keller shook his head. "I think I must have left by then. Between the police wanting to arrest Brittney and . . . well, the tiff she had with you"—he glanced at Dixie—"I left early."

"Well, the dirt on the street is that Dixon Vannover was leaving his wife to be with Naomi, who was . . . supposedly . . . carrying his baby."

Warren stared speechless for several moments, but eventually he chuckled. "Well, that's outrageous. Naomi couldn't be pregnant."

"We know, the coroner confirmed that she wasn't, but if Dixon Vannover thought she was . . . well, he might have gotten violent."

"I see." Warren stared. "But did he have the opportunity to murder her?"

"We know June followed him to the dog show, so he was there."

"Of course, the police will need to investigate and verify everything," I said, suddenly feeling a need to hedge my bets. I believed June Vannover was telling the truth when she said she followed her husband to the dog show, but just because she said it didn't make it true.

We chatted a bit longer but didn't want to overstay our welcome. So we made our excuses and left. Dixie stopped by her house to pick up a salad and a cake that Mrs. Huntington had prepared for tonight.

"I didn't realize you lived so close to the Kellers."

"To be honest, I didn't either, until I was out walking the girls and ran across Warren Keller hiking."

"Do you suppose Naomi knew?"

"I'm sure she did. She wasn't stupid. The dog show circuit is a small world. I find it hard to believe she didn't know where I lived."

Dixie drove us down the mountain. While I kept my eyes closed tightly and my hand on the door's armrest, I barely pushed my foot through my imaginary brake and only recited one rosary. I was making progress.

Back down in civilization, we stopped by a chain store known for crafts, and I ordered a frame for my painting. The canvas was large, but it was a standard size, and they had a dark frame that complemented the leaf beautifully.

Back home, I wasn't surprised to find Red's truck. When we got out, I heard the lawnmower and knew he was occupied. Stephanie was inside, keeping the dogs entertained, which wasn't an easy task. When we went outside, I was surprised to see Joe and David in the corner of the yard, installing a large cedar gazebo that I had admired for months.

Stephanie placed an arm around my shoulders. "We wanted to surprise you." She looked closely in my eyes. "You like it, right?"

I was so shocked and overwhelmed that I couldn't speak and merely stood there blubbering. I hugged Stephanie as tight as I could. When I managed to find my words, I mumbled, "I love it."

Stephanie was crying, and Red, David, and Joe stood, staring back at us with fear in their eyes. Eventually, Dixie waved. "She loves it."

The guys breathed a sigh of relief. David came forward and hugged me. "I'm so glad you like it. I threatened to pummel him if we went to all this work and then had to take it out."

I squeezed him. "I love it."

Red finished mowing the grass around the gazebo and took a defensive stance. "Please, tell me this is the one you wanted. I don't want to face the wrath of your kids if I got it wrong."

I hugged him. "You got it absolutely right." I could feel his muscles relax. After a few moments, he pulled away. "I smell horrible."

I smiled through my tears. "Thank you."

I walked over to my new gazebo. "Can I go in?"

"Absolutely." David and Joe took me inside.

"How on earth did you manage to get this installed today?"

Red pointed to Joe. "He did the majority of the work."

I walked over and gave him a big hug. "Thank you!"

"The hardest part was getting the foundation done, but the builders took care of most of that for us. It was pretty easy."

We spent quite a lot of time admiring the new gazebo until the rest of the guests arrived. Each new arrival meant a trip to the gazebo. The dogs seemed to enjoy it too.

When everyone had seen and given their stamp of approval on the new addition, we sat down to eat. Thankfully, Stephanie and Dixie hadn't been idle while I was giving tours; they had ordered several large pizzas.

Despite the chaos of twelve adults and eleven dogs, the dinner went surprisingly well. The adults were able to comfortably enjoy our gourmet cuisine, while the dogs enjoyed grilled hot dogs. When we were stuffed, the dogs lay down near their owners' feet, and we started our meeting.

My bombshell about Dixon Vannover was the highlight.

I looked to Dixie. "Does your club have video cameras around the building so we can confirm that Vannover was actually at the dog club at the time of the murder?"

"No, but lots of the competitors make videos. Maybe someone managed to capture him. Several of the members have already uploaded their videos to our website." She pulled out her phone and swiped a few times. "I'll send out an e-mail asking for all the videos."

"That would be great. We need to collect all the videos we can that were taken near the RV on Saturday."

The only other item of interest came from David, who managed to find an extremely chatty volunteer who swore Dixon Vannover's opponents were trying to destroy his good character by accusing him of womanizing.

"The thing is, she was so adamant that he couldn't possibly have done it, that she brought up rumors I hadn't even heard of."

"Like what?" Red asked.

"Not only did she deny that Dixon Vannover had had any extramarital affairs, she also denied the accusations that he liked to dress up in women's clothes."

"So Dixon Vannover is a transvestite?"

"I don't think he is openly trans."

B.J. sipped her beer. "To each his own. 'Live and let live' is my motto."

"Mine too," David said, "but it flies against the attitudes of his base constituency and some of the things on his platform." He pulled out a brochure from Vannover's campaign and passed it around.

I read several of his key beliefs and felt myself getting angry. I passed the brochure. "That's very narrow-minded." I glanced at my son. "I'm so sorry I asked you to volunteer there."

David grinned. "Well, I have to admit the first day grated on my nerves. However, today I was prepared."

Something in the way he looked made me ask, "What did you do?"

He chuckled. "Well, when I heard about his penchant for dressing up, I called my girlfriend, the hacker."

Red scowled. "Am I going to regret hearing this?"

Madison smiled. "You might want to cover your ears."

Red didn't cover his ears, but he frowned as he listened.

Madison said, "Dixon Vannover likes himself too much not to have taken pictures of himself in drag."

"Tell me you didn't use TBI resources to hack a suspect's files," Red said, glaring.

"Of course not." Madison shook her head. "I didn't have to. All I did was search the Internet. Heck, anybody could have done it. I knew that jerk wouldn't be bright enough to know that just because you delete a photo in a post doesn't mean you've deleted it completely."

David made a few swipes across his cell phone and showed us a video of Dixon Vannover wearing a black wig and singing "It's Raining Men" in full drag.

Monica Jill stared in shocked surprise. "Oh my God. Look at his legs."

"Girl, how can you look at his legs with all that shimmying going on?" B.J. asked.

We laughed at the video until I felt guilty. "I'm torn. I mean, if he wants to dress in drag, that's certainly his right."

"True," David said. "Honestly, if he weren't such a huge hypocrite, I wouldn't have been tempted to upload this to every social media site I could find."

I gasped. But David held up a hand. "I said I was tempted to upload it. In the end, I couldn't do it." He swiped his phone and put it away. "I think the man is a hypocritical jerk with the emotional intelligence of a goldfish, but . . . I don't believe in dirty politics either."

I reached across and gave my son a kiss. "I'm proud of you, honey. Whether he wins or loses his election, I hope that the decision will be made based on the issues and not . . . his personal life."

"Is there any more pizza inside?" Monica Jill said. "I'm starving." She hurried to the kitchen.

When she was gone, B.J. leaned across the table. "Have you noticed that she's eating like a condemned man on death row?"

Mai smiled. "Maybe she's been working out?"

B.J.'s face said that was highly unlikely.

"Maybe she missed lunch," Stephanie said.

"I'm sure carting potential home buyers around all day can be exhausting," I said, "and she has to go when her clients and the house are available. I remember when I was looking for this place, we must have seen at least fifty houses." I glanced at Dixie, who had been there for almost all of them.

"It's a buyer's market, and I'm sure she's been working nonstop."

Dr. Morgan asked, "Did she ever get checked out by her doctor?"

"She went this morning," B.J. said. "She's waiting for all of the results to come back." B.J. squinted at the doctor. "Why? You don't think she's got a brain tumor, do you?"

Dr. Morgan shook his head. "I doubt very seriously if she has a brain tumor. It could be anything from dehydration to high blood pressure. However, I wouldn't jump to any conclusions."

Monica Jill came back with a plate loaded with salad and two more slices of pizza. "Who's jumping to conclusions?"

We were saved from responding when Red's phone rang, and he stepped away to take the call in private. Dixie adroitly changed the subject by bringing up the housewarming, which got us all talking about the plans for the weekend. After a few moments, Red rejoined the group. Despite his stoic expression, I knew by the clenching of his jaw that something was wrong.

"What happened?" I asked.

"That was Officer Lewis. Dixon Vannover was just found . . . murdered."

Chapter 19

We had a million questions, but Red didn't have any answers. All he knew was that Dixon had been strangled. He said he needed to go and made a quick exit, promising to call me later. Joe promised to make sure that Steve Austin, Red's dog, made it home safely.

"Glad I deleted that video now," David said.

We tried to comfort him, but I knew the best thing we could do was to get busy. "This is horrible. Just because none of us liked him doesn't mean we wanted him dead."

"I suppose this rules him out as a suspect," Beau said.

"I'd say that's a good assumption. Chances are rare that there are two stranglers out there."

"So now we need to figure out who murdered Naomi Keller and Dixon Vannover," Dr. Morgan said.

"I'm worried about June," Dixie said.

"That poor woman sells her first painting and loses her husband on the same day," Monica Jill said.

I glanced at Dixie. "Casserole?"

She nodded. "Casserole."

"Any chance June killed them both?" Madison asked.

We stared.

"I suppose it's possible," I said. "Although . . . she seemed to worship the man."

"True, but he was a lying womanizer," B.J. said. "Besides, how do we know that June Vannover is the innocent she claims to be?"

"You mean like Dr. Jekyll and Mr. Hyde?"

"Maybe June Vannover is meek and mild when she's sober, but once she's wasted, she becomes a totally different person."

Something in the way she spoke made me ask, "Are you speaking from experience?"

She took a deep breath. "My ex-husband was like that. When he was sober, he was the perfect husband. He was kind, thoughtful, romantic, and . . . sweet." She shook her head. "But once he got drunk, he became mean and abusive."

"I didn't know alcohol could do that," Monica Jill said. "I always thought liquor amplified your personality rather than changed it altogether."

"Well, that's not how it worked with Richard. I put up with it for a few years. He always promised that he was going to stop drinking, but he couldn't."

Monica Jill reached out and touched her friend's arm. "I had no idea."

"Why should you? We've been divorced for almost ten years now." She shrugged. "I've moved on. He's moved on too. Now he's remarried and some other woman's problem, but just because this June Vannover seemed nice when you met her doesn't mean she's that way all the time."

"That's true, Mom," Stephanie said. "You did say you thought she wasn't a stranger to alcohol."

"That was just my first thought. I'm certainly no expert."

"Well, your instincts are usually pretty good," Joe said.

I thought for a few moments. "You're all right. I guess I feel sorry for her, so I don't want her to be guilty. The facts are that she was angry with Naomi Keller. She believed she was having an affair with her husband and that he planned to leave her."

"And Naomi Keller ended up dead," B.J. said.

"Strangled to death," Dixie added.

"Next thing we know, June's husband ends up dead," Monica Jill said.

"Strangled to death," Stephanie said.

I held up my hands. "Okay, June Vannover stays on the list."

B.J. raised an eyebrow. "Stays on the list? June Vannover needs to be at the top of the list."

"Okay, but we can't eliminate our other suspects. There's still Britney Keller." I glanced around the table and noted that the others nodded their agreement, although reluctantly.

"There's also Warren Keller," Dixie said. "His motive is just as strong as June's. Naomi was his wife."

"Plus Dixon Vannover was diddling not only his wife, but his daughter too," Madison said.

I glanced around. "Anyone else?"

"That's enough for now, don't you think?" Dixie said.

We talked about our next steps. Joe hadn't been able to visit the Greyhound rescue, but he promised he would do so tomorrow. Dixie and I planned to take a casserole to June Vannover. Mai was also planning to visit the rescue to get more info on Brittany Keller. Theodore Jordan was going to court, but Stephanie was going to ask around at the pub and the courthouse.

"I was supposed to meet with Dixon Vannover tomorrow morning," Beau said, "but . . . now I don't have an assignment."

"I think you and David should still go to the campaign site," I said. "The workers may have some insight that might help."

David narrowed his eyes. "What kind of insight?"

"Did he have an argument with someone? Maybe someone heard that he was going to meet with one of our suspects. Look, I doubt that we're going to find a note on the floor saying, 'Meet killer at seven p.m.,' but you never know what someone heard. There's bound to be a lot of emotions, and maybe someone will let something slip that we can use later."

David nodded. "Got it."

"You want us to just listen and see if there's something that will help tie these murders together," Beau said.

"Yes," I said. "We don't have a lot to go on, except now we have one more dead body."

Monica Jill patted my arm. "Hopefully, we also have one less suspect."

Later, when I was in bed, I wondered if Monica Jill was right. Did we have one less suspect? Were we even looking in the right direction? I tried to think through what I knew about Naomi Keller and Dixon Vannover. In my gut, I didn't believe the murders were unrelated. So if they were related, what did the two people have in common? They were lovers. That meant there were two spouses who might have wanted one of them dead, but would either June Vannover or Warren Keller want both of them dead? Try as I might, the only person I could imagine who would want to see both of them dead was Brittany Keller. If she was in love with Dixon Vannover and he had jilted her, then she might be angry enough to want him dead. *If I can't have him, then no one can* may seem clichéd, but newspapers were filled with stories of an injured lover with that mentality. Plus, she hated her stepmother. The fact that her lover tossed her aside for her stepmother had to be like pouring salt into an open wound. After delivering my casserole to June Vannover, I needed to make my way to the Greyhound rescue.

I sat up in bed. "My goodness. I need to make a casserole."

Chapter 20

A quick text message to Dixie helped me realize that not only did I not need to attempt to make a casserole in the middle of the night, but that Mrs. Huntington had us both covered. So I was able to sleep.

On Wednesday, I was so excited to go to work, I didn't need my alarm clock or my poodle to wake me up. In fact, Aggie gave me a sideways glance when I scooped her and Rex up to go outside. Even Lucky took a few extra stretches before he trotted outside too. Once the four-legged creatures had tended to the call of nature, I was able to grab a cup of coffee and tend to my own needs.

I took extra care getting dressed and even took extra time to curl my hair and apply makeup. When I was dressed, I found David and Stephanie sitting outside drinking coffee. Both had gone out after our meeting and come home in the early hours of the morning, so neither were looking exactly chipper.

"Good morning," I sang.

David grunted and Stephanie gave me a look that implied my happy disposition wasn't appreciated at this hour of the morning. Nevertheless, I was bound and determined to enjoy this day and merely sipped my coffee in the beauty of the morning.

Stephanie glared. "Who are you and what have you done with our mother?"

"Very funny."

David grinned. "I was just about to check the back of your neck for pods."

"Ha ha. Who knew I had such amusing offspring?"

"You do seem to be in surprisingly good humor this morning," Stephanie said. "What's up?"

"It's my first day at work as a real employee."

"I completely forgot." Stephanie hugged me. "Congratulations, Mom."

"Thank you. It's my first real job in"—I glanced at David—"over twenty years." I had given up my job as a CPA when he was born and worked in my husband's used-car dealership. When his business started doing well, he hired someone to do the bookkeeping so I could stay home and focus on raising our children. I had kept my CPA license over the years but rarely got to use it. "I feel . . . independent." I smiled. "I had no idea how important it was to me to know that I could take care of myself." I took a deep breath. "Moving wasn't easy. In fact, it was rather scary, but I wanted . . . needed a fresh start, and this confirms that I made the right decision." I choked up.

"Mom, we're both so proud of you," Stephanie said, and she leaned over and hugged me.

After a few moments, I pulled away. "I'm going to need to redo my makeup if I don't stop blubbering like a baby."

"You deserve a little blubber," David said. "However, if you don't want to be late on your first day, we'd better get a move on."

David drove me to work, and I was pleasantly surprised that in addition to the two vases of flowers I'd received yesterday, there was also a lovely plaque outside my door with my name and title. I almost teared up again but avoided making a fool of myself in front of Jacob and Linda Kay, who were standing there to welcome me.

After I put away my purse, I joined my coworkers for pastries and coffee in Linda Kay's office.

I wasn't surprised when Linda Kay said, "We'll get your paperwork signed and sent to Human Resources, but first we're hoping you can fill us in on the dirt about Dixon Vannover's murder."

"I hate to disappoint you, but all I know is that Red got a call last night that Vannover had been strangled."

"Just like Naomi Keller?" Jacob asked.

"As far as I know, but he didn't say how it was done."

"Maybe it was June?"

I stared. "What makes you say that?"

"I've just been imagining what happened between her and Dixon when he got home yesterday and found out she was planning to leave him."

I spewed my coffee. "She what?"

Jacob grabbed a few napkins and helped me wipe up the mess from the table, although my carefully planned first-day-as-a-permanent-employee outfit was ruined. "I thought you knew."

I shook my head. "She didn't mention anything about leaving her husband when I was there."

"I bought three of her paintings," Linda Kay said and pointed to several canvases in a corner that I had missed while distracted by pastries.

"I bought two, and then we took about twenty on consignment," Jacob said. He finished cleaning, sat down.

"Consignment?" I asked.

Linda Kay nodded. "Sara Jane Hopewell was a huge patron of the arts and she often sponsored art showings to promote local artists. We have an arrangement with several of the local art galleries and occasionally host exhibits for new artists."

"I don't think I've ever thought about the museum selling art. Do you do that?"

"Do *we* do that." Linda Kay's smile reminded me that I was now part of the museum. "It's not something we do often. The AAMD has traditionally frowned on museums selling art from their permanent collections."

"What's the AAMD?" I asked.

"It's the Association of Art Museum Directors."

Jacob held his head in the air and pushed his nose up with his finger. "Snobs who would rather see a museum place buckets on the floor to catch rain dripping through a leaky roof than allow a museum to sell a few paintings to pay to get the roof repaired."

Linda Kay tsked. "That's not fair. The AAMD has reasons for their actions, but given the declining revenue that museums have had in recent years, it's really forced change." She looked as though she were remembering a different time, but quickly shook herself and returned to the present. "Regardless, June Vannover's paintings weren't part of our permanent collection. It's no different than selling a reproduction of the Mona Lisa in the gift shop, except the museum will get a commission."

Jacob pulled out a pen and wrote on a napkin. "You paid two hundred for your painting. I paid five hundred for the two I bought."

"My total was eight hundred," Linda Kay said.

"That's fifteen hundred just from the three of us. Plus, we're going to arrange a showing at the museum, and she could easily make six figures if we display the art properly and invite the right buyers."

Thankfully, I had put my cup down, so I only dropped a pastry this time. "Six figures? Are you serious?"

"Oh, yes," Linda Kay said. "She's very talented. When you sent me those photos, I got chills. That's why I sent Jacob over there immediately to snatch up those paintings." She looked sheepish. "I have to confess I was anxious to get there before she signed with an agent because the price would be triple what we paid."

"Now I feel so guilty for only giving her two hundred dollars," I said. "I like a bargain just like everyone, but I certainly don't want to take advantage of her."

Linda Kay patted my knee. "Didn't you say she was only going to charge you fifty dollars?"

I nodded.

"Then you weren't taking advantage of her. Besides, you're an accountant, not an art valuation expert, so stop worrying."

I turned to Jacob. "Did she really say she planned to leave her husband?"

"Yeah. She was shocked that we were interested in her art. She said Dixon told her she didn't have any talent and that no one would ever pay more than two dollars for it."

"But what were her exact words?"

He thought for a moment. "Well, she was stunned by the checks and not really talking to me. In fact, she was talking to herself, but she said, 'Maybe Lilly was right. It's not too late. I can support myself without Dixon. I can start over. Have children. Find my happy place.'" He shrugged. "I'm not sure those were her exact words, but that was it more or less."

I tried to think of something else, but June Vannover's words kept coming back to me. Just because she wanted to start over without her husband didn't mean she had killed him. Chances were good she meant divorce, not murder. Jacob obviously thought that's what she meant. However, I wasn't sure that the police would feel the same way. In fact, I was pretty sure there was at least one TBI officer who might interpret those words differently.

Chapter 21

Linda Kay walked me through the job description for my position, including salary and benefits. I knew I'd never get rich working for a nonprofit, and the salary she offered confirmed that. However, for me, it wasn't about the dollar amount. I still had some money left from selling my house in Indiana, and I wasn't extravagant, so it would be more than enough for me and two poodles. No, it wasn't the money, but the fact that I now had roots.

After I signed my offer letter, I met with Human Resources and filled out my tax papers. When I was legally and officially an employee, I sat at my desk, looked out the window onto the Tennessee River, and cried. I said a prayer of thanks to Miss Florrie, and then I dried my eyes, pulled out my laptop, and got back to work.

Several hours later, I jumped when Jacob knocked on my door. "I'm heading home." I glanced at my watch. It was after five, and Dixie would be here to pick me up in just a matter of minutes.

"Thank you for everything," I said. "I'll see you tomorrow." I waved at Jacob as he walked down the hall. "Tell your mom I said hello."

He grunted a reply, and then I heard the elevator doors close. I shut down my laptop and hurried downstairs. I saw Dixie's Lexus in the visitor parking space and hurried over.

"I'm sorry. Have you been waiting long?"

"Not at all." She pulled out onto the narrow street in front of the museum and then made her way onto one of the interstates that crisscrossed the downtown area.

On the short drive to the Vannover estate, I filled Dixie in on what I'd learned from Linda Kay and Jacob.

"I wish I'd gotten one of those paintings before Jacob arrived," Dixie said. "She may have more, but I'm sure he took the best ones."

"Well, you can always buy one from the museum when she has her showing."

"I'm sorry. I really was listening to what you said about her 'dumping' her husband. I'm sure you're right and that she was just planning to leave him, but . . . well, I don't know if Red would agree."

"I've been thinking the same thing."

She pulled up to the gated community, and we lucked out. The gate was open, so she drove to the house. There were several cars already there.

"I didn't ask Red where the body was found," I said. "I wonder . . ."

"I suppose they'll let us leave our food and give condolences if nothing else." She got out of the car, opened the back door, and handed me a casserole, while she took in a plate of brownies. "I don't know if Dixon Vannover had a lot of family, but June can take the food to her neighbors if she has too much."

We walked up to the front door. Just as we were about to ring the doorbell, the door opened and June Vannover and a hunk of a man with rock-solid good looks that reminded me of Clark Kent came out.

"Oh . . . Lilly and Dixie." June tried to hug us, but it was awkward with the food. "How nice of you two to bring food." She glanced at the man. "Paul, these are my friends, Lilly Ann Echosby and Dixie Jefferson. This is Paul Redburn, my attorney."

We nodded in lieu of shaking hands, and I tried not to stare at his uncanny resemblance to Superman's alter ego.

"Forgive my manners. Please, come in. The house is overrun with police, and I just can't stand it anymore. I have to get out of here or I'll scream." Her housekeeper came around the corner. "Mary, would you please take these to the kitchen?"

Mary relieved us of both items with the skill born from years of serving others and marched off to the kitchen before we could offer to help.

June smiled. "Mary's been in a huff all day with the police rummaging through the house and dusting that black powder all over looking for fingerprints or clues." She sighed. "I told her she should take the day off and come back when they're done, but she refuses to leave the house unattended." She laughed. "I think she believes they'll make off with the good silverware if she's not here to watch them like a hawk."

"June, we wanted to give our condolences and let you know that if there is anything we can do to help, please don't hesitate to let us know," Dixie said.

"Thank you. I appreciate that, but you've already done so much."

Dixie and I exchanged looks, and I saw the same puzzled expression on her face that I knew must have been on my own. "I'm not sure what you mean," I said.

"Dixie introduced you to me, and then . . . you not only bought my first painting, but you called your friends at the Hopewell, and they bought so many paintings." She got choked up. "I can't even remember how many, and they're going to help me arrange a showing. I just . . ." She fanned her face and tried to keep the tears from falling.

"You made all of those amazing paintings yourself. All I did was make a phone call." I hugged her. Before we pulled apart, she whispered, "I'm going to take your advice and tell the truth."

When we separated, Dixie, June, and I all needed handkerchiefs.

"Now that we've ruined our makeup," I said, "we should probably let you two go."

June hesitated, but Paul Redburn flashed a dazzling smile, and she agreed, but not without first arranging for us to meet for lunch one day next week.

Back in the car, we headed downtown to the Greyhound rescue.

"What did you think of Superman?" Dixie asked.

"I tried not to stare, but he looked so much like Clark Kent that I just couldn't help myself." I turned in my seat so I could see Dixie's face. "Do you think there's something going on there?"

She hesitated. "I've known June Vannover for years. She's always been such a mouse. A week ago, I'd have staked my life that she'd never even glanced in the direction of another man. For the longest time, I thought she practically worshipped Dixon. However, I think Superman may have some other ideas."

"I got the same impression, and I hope it works out for them."

"You're thinking about you and Red, aren't you?"

I couldn't stop myself from grinning. "I suppose so." I leaned back on the seat. "Sometimes I just want to pinch myself. I can't believe I'm living in this beautiful city."

Dixie drove around an area of town the locals called the ridge cut. It's where the interstate does a forty-five-degree turn and provides an amazing look at the city, especially when the sun sets behind the mountains and rays of red, orange, and deep purple and the sparkle of white lights are the only illumination.

I gazed out over Chattanooga, which I now felt was home. "Plus I have friends." I stared at her. "There's you and everyone from the dog club,

Aggie and Rex and . . . Red." I took a deep breath. "I didn't realize how lonely I was before, especially after Stephanie and David left, but now my life is just so full that I'm almost afraid."

She reached a hand across and patted my leg. "I know what you mean. It's been wonderful having you so close. Now you've got a permanent job, a wonderful boyfriend who adores you, and you're buying a house."

"Oh, I almost forgot, I have the inspection tomorrow and have to remember to call the bank and wire the money to the title company." I pulled out my phone and typed a reminder for myself. "What did we do before cell phones?"

Dixie pulled off the interstate. "I have no idea."

We chatted while Dixie navigated the city traffic toward downtown. Thankfully, we were going against city workers who were heading for the interstate to make their way to the suburbs, but there was still quite a bit of traffic between cars, buses, and tourists riding the blue-and lime-green electric bicycles the city had added to reduce carbon emissions while promoting exercise and outdoor enjoyment. Eventually, we saw the building for the Greyhound rescue, which was located close to the Choo-Choo Hotel. There was very limited parking near the rescue, and Dixie had to circle the block. When she turned the corner across from the Choo-Choo, I saw a small, stand-alone brick building on a corner lot. It was dilapidated, with graffiti sprayed all over the exterior. The building had been an automotive garage at some point in its past life. "Stop."

Dixie pulled into the parking lot. "What?"

"That building would make a great doggie day care for tourists and busy city workers."

Dixie rolled her eyes. "Et tu, Brute?"

"That building is perfect." I opened the car door and got out, knowing curiosity would make her follow me.

I peeked through the window at the inside and felt her next to me before she spoke. "This place looks horrible."

"It does, but it's a great location." The building was off a side street. Many of the old brownstone storefront buildings that had fallen into disrepair were being renovated and turned into trendy shops, restaurants, and coffee shops. The city had torn down the older homes and was building small, single-family homes.

The area behind the building was an empty lot that was long and too narrow to build on. "You could probably buy that lot too for a dog run, but isn't there a dog park near here?"

Dixie appeared deep in thought. "Actually, there is. It's a few blocks that way." She pointed, and I squinted around a couple of houses and saw the sign. "I'd forgotten about the dog park." She walked around the building. "You know, this place might actually have some potential."

We walked around the building multiple times, peeking into the windows that hadn't been boarded up. "I could probably take some of this parking lot and convert it into more green space too."

We chatted about possible changes until we were both excited about the possibilities. Dixie jotted down the name and telephone number of the real estate firm handling the sale, and we got back in the car. Before she pulled away, she sent the information to Monica Jill. This time, we were able to find a parking space behind the building. Dixie pulled in, and we went inside.

I'm not sure what I expected the headquarters of a dog rescue organization to look like, but this one didn't fit any of those boxes. The building was basically an office where the workers provided brochures on the sins of dog racing and the benefits of the Greyhound as a pet. There were two Greyhounds and a white cat curled up together on an old sofa placed against one of the walls. The sleek, majestic animals lifted their heads as we walked in but, deeming us unworthy of further scrutiny, put them back down and continued their naps.

"I've heard Greyhounds described as couch potatoes, but this is taking things a bit far," I whispered to Dixie.

She smiled, walked over to the dogs, and squatted down and offered her hand. The animals sniffed her, and their tails immediately began to wag, pounding the sofa like metronomes. Dixie scratched each dog behind the ear, causing the beat of the tail wags to increase and their eyes to roll back in their heads. She cooed and whispered compliments in the voice understood by babies and dogs.

After a few moments, a door near the back opened, and Brittney Keller walked out.

"I'm sorry. I didn't realize anyone was here." She walked forward and extended a hand. "I see you've already met our greeters."

I shook her hand and allowed Dixie time to finish her Greyhound conversation.

"Hello, my name is Lilly Ann Echosby, and this . . ."—I glanced toward Dixie, who had wrapped up her greeting with the hounds.

"Dixie Jefferson," Brittney Keller said. "Dog trainer, judge, and my stepmother's nemesis."

I wasn't sure how to take that, and based on Dixie's face, I don't think she was quite sure either.

Brittney Keller must have picked up on it because she quickly added, "Hey, sorry. No insult intended. Frankly, any enemy of my stepmonster is a friend of mine."

"What's that ancient proverb? *The enemy of my enemy is my friend.*"

I knew Dixie quoted literature and movies when she was nervous, but I thought this seemed fitting, as the same thing had gone through my mind. "At the risk of stating the obvious, you really didn't like your stepmother very much, did you?"

She folded her arms across her chest. "What was your first clue?"

"The syrup you slung at her at the dog club," I said.

"Along with the curses you flung at her as you were being dragged out of the building," Dixie added.

She laughed. "Yeah, well, let's just say that Naomi and I weren't exactly close. So I certainly wasn't going to pass up an opportunity to publicly humiliate her." She frowned. "But, surely, you two didn't come here just to talk about how much I hated my stepmother. How can I help you?"

I waited for Dixie to respond. She was so much better at thinking on her feet. "First, we came to offer our condolences. We visited your father yesterday, and he seemed devastated. We dropped off some food, but is there anything either of you need? Anything we can do?"

For an instant, I noticed the first genuine sympathy from Brittney Keller. She may not have cared for her stepmother, but she obviously cared very strongly for her dad. "Thank you. Dad is devastated. He just sits around drinking and staring at that stupid award she got at the dog show and crying." She huffed. "I have no idea why, but for some reason he loved that witch. No accounting for taste."

"I haven't heard when the visitation will be. I'd like to go and pay my respects."

Brittney gave Dixie a cocky stare. "I didn't think you and the Wicked Witch of East Tennessee were that tight. Didn't you punch her out the other day?" She grinned and leaned forward. "Nice job, by the way."

Dixie blushed. "I'm sorry about that. I should have been able to control my temper, but . . . well, it's something that I definitely regret."

She *tsk*ed. "Pity. I often wondered if Stepmomzilla and I mightn't have gotten along a lot better if we'd been allowed to have a knock-down, drag-out fight." She sighed and walked to her desk, where she picked up a cell phone. After a few swipes, she said, "Visitation is tomorrow at noon, and the funeral will immediately follow." She gave Dixie the name of the funeral home and then tossed the phone back on her desk. "Needless to say, I won't be attending, but you knock yourself out. Is that all?"

"This building isn't what I expected," I said. "I guess I was envisioning something more . . . dog-friendly."

"Come with me." She led us back through the door where she had entered, and the back of the building was bright and open. The building was long. "We have almost two-thousand square feet of indoor space equipped with three-quarter-inch RB rubber matting, sold as Tenderfoot flooring. It provides cushioning, traction, joint protection, and shock absorption." There was a door at the back of the building that led to a larger fenced area. "This is another two thousand square feet of outdoor space that's equipped with awnings for shaded play and a small pool."

The outdoor area appeared to have been part of the original building, with the roof removed to expose the area to the sunlight.

Dixie pointed to the ceilings. "That's pretty ingenious."

"The back of the building was in bad shape. The roof had collapsed, and there was a tree growing through the floor. Rather than spending tons of money to demolish and rebuild, we decided to salvage the walls, which were in good shape, and forget the roof. We shored up the front of the building and left the back."

Brittney was obviously pleased with what they'd done.

However, I was still slightly confused. "Where are the dogs? I mean, this is a rescue, right?"

"We've re-homed all of the dogs we had, and we're moving to Florida to help with re-homing all of the former racing Greyhounds." She glanced around. "It's a pity. I'm going to miss this place."

Dixie asked. "What's going to happen to this building?"

"We're going to try and sell it, but . . . I'm sure whoever buys it will just tear it down and build another yuppy pub, coffee bar or condos."

"I've read about the Hounds and Heroes. Don't they meet here?"

She shook her head. "Hounds and Heroes is an organization that trains retired Greyhounds for military service men and women, but all of the work is done through volunteers and foster pet parents."

We talked a bit more and went back inside to the office area. We took some of the brochures and then made our exit.

Back in the car, Dixie's phone rang. "This is B.J." She swiped the phone. "Hello—"

"Monica Jill's having a meltdown," B.J. said. "I'm going to need some backup. She wouldn't give us any details but provided an address in Charleston, Tennessee."

I looked at Dixie. "What do you think is wrong?"

"I don't know, but wasn't today the day that Monica Jill was supposed to get her results back on those tests?"

We stared at each other for several moments, and then Dixie put the pedal to the metal and practically flew down the interstate. Then she took the winding country roads at a speed that left me gasping for breath and clutching the door armrest as we bounced and jostled. We passed horses, cows, turkeys, and what appeared to be a llama on our way into the backwoods, but eventually we arrived at a newly constructed home on the river. B.J. and Dr. Morgan's cars were already in the driveway. We pulled up behind them and hurried to the door.

B.J. flung the door open. "Come in. Y'all gonna need to hear this yourself."

We hurried inside and found Monica Jill lying facedown on the floor. She had her arms sprawled out.

"What's wrong?" Dixie asked Dr. Morgan, who was standing nearby with a smile. He picked up a paper from the dining room table and handed it to her.

I stood over Dixie's shoulder and read.

Congratulations on your pregnancy.

Chapter 22

"She's pregnant?" we said together.

Dr. Morgan nodded. "I suspected as much, but . . ."

Monica Jill was still on the floor. "Don't you dare say those words to me. I refuse to believe this. I absolutely cannot be pregnant."

B.J. walked over to the counter and took a bottle of wine. She poured herself a glass. "This explains why you passed out and have been eating like a horse."

"I have not been eating like a horse. And how dare you drink alcohol in front of me when you know I can't have any."

B.J. smirked. "I'm doing this for you. Your nerves are shot, so I'm just trying to help you."

"How is your drinking wine helping my nerves?"

"It's keeping me from killing you." She sipped her wine.

Monica Jill kicked and beat her feet on the floor. "This isn't fair. It's not fair. I can't be pregnant. I just can't."

I turned to B.J. "How long has she been like this?"

"Since she left the doctor's office. She called me to come get her, and she's been throwing a first-rate tantrum since we arrived."

Dr. Morgan sipped his wine. "I'm not really sure why I'm here."

"Moral support," B.J. said.

"I don't need moral support," Monica Jill said. "I need a drink."

"I wasn't talking about you," B.J. said. "I've been listening to this wailing and whining and gnashing of teeth all day, and my nerves are shot. It's someone else's turn." She grabbed the bottle and walked through the living room out onto the large screened porch that overlooked the river.

Dr. Morgan smiled. "I think I'll join her."

Dixie and I walked to the living room and looked down at Monica Jill. "How far along?" Dixie asked.

"I have no idea. I never got beyond the first lines on that paper." She rolled over onto her back. "I kept thinking it has to be wrong. I'm too old for this. My daughter is grown and living in another state. We're empty nesters. We're supposed to be traveling and enjoying life. I should be getting ready for grandchildren, not having a baby."

"I'm going to the bathroom," I said. "Where . . ."

Monica Jill, normally a grand hostess, barely moved. She merely pointed down a hall.

I walked until I found a door, which I assumed was the bathroom, and I was pleased to know I had guessed right. In typical Monica Jill fashion, the room was decorated in the popular contemporary rustic style that I'd seen on HGTV design shows. The only surprise was that the counter and the trash can were littered with boxes, which was out of character for my meticulous friend. Closer inspection of the boxes showed them to be various makes and brands of home pregnancy tests.

Back in the living room, I asked, "So you didn't trust the results from the doctor?"

Monica Jill turned her head to glare at me. "Would you?"

I worked to keep from laughing. "How many pregnancy tests did you take?"

She shook her head. "I don't know. Twenty-five . . . thirty."

Dixie snorted.

"Don't you laugh at me, Scarlet Jefferson. If you got some report saying you were pregnant in your forties, you'd do the same thing."

I sat down on the sofa. "Have you told your husband?"

She shook her head. "I can't. I just can't. We just paid off both our house and this river house. He was so excited about traveling and seeing the world." She turned to look at me. "How can I tell him that he can just kiss that dream good-bye. We're going to be changing diapers and getting up in the middle of the night and . . . paying for day care, and now we're going to need to put another child through college."

"All that's true, but you're going to have a baby. You're going to get to watch it grow up and take its first steps. You get to be there for its first words and see the look in his . . . or her eyes when they recognize your face and smile."

She let out a heavy sigh. "But . . . I'm old."

"You're mature, not old." I chuckled. "You're also wiser and more financially prepared for a baby."

"What's the real problem?" Dixie asked.

She paused. "I'm scared."

"That's understandable, but you know *God is faithful, who will not suffer you to be tempted above that ye are able; but will with the temptation also make a way to escape, that ye may be able to bear it.*"

Monica Jill smiled. "First Corinthians, ten thirteen."

I hadn't noticed that B.J. had joined us until she spoke. "Plus, you have us for support."

Jac had been lying at his mistress's side but took that opportunity to give her face a lick before he circled three times and then curled up by her face. If she turned her head in his direction, they were nose to nose.

"Even Jac will help you through this," Dixie said.

"Now get your butt up off the floor," B.J. ordered. "I'm hungry. What do you have to eat?"

Whether at the sound of the word *eat* or the time of day, Monica Jill's stomach let out a large growl, and we all laughed.

"I guess I am a bit hungry." She sat up. "I have a lasagna in the fridge."

B.J. extended a hand to help her friend off the floor. "Why do you have a lasagna in the fridge? Were you expecting company?"

"I was planning to take it to either June Vannover or Warren Keller. I hadn't decided yet, but I can always make them another one."

"I love the Southern casserole thing," I said.

"Every Southern girl was raised to take food when someone dies." Monica Jill said from the kitchen as she put the large dish into the oven. She opened the freezer and removed a bag with frozen garlic bread and placed it on the counter, and then she took out ingredients for a salad.

B.J. retrieved plates from a cabinet. "In Black families, we tend to bring fried chicken more than casseroles. When my mom passed, we had so much chicken I couldn't look at a bird for two months."

It didn't take long before the kitchen smelled of tomatoes, garlic, and herbs. We all filled our plates with salad and headed to the screened porch to eat and enjoy the peaceful sounds of the river. While we ate, Dixie and I shared everything from our encounter with June Vannover and her hunky attorney to our conversation with Brittney Keller.

B.J. sipped her wine. "Check this out. I found out that Warren Keller did have an insurance policy on Naomi. Actually, they each had policies, but since Warren is still alive, I'm going to just focus on Naomi's. He had a policy on Naomi for a million dollars."

"A million dollars?" we all repeated.

"Seems high to me," I said.

"Who's the beneficiary?" Dr. Morgan asked.

B.J. leaned forward. "Here's the extra-suspicious part. Both of them listed Brittney Keller as beneficiary." She gave us a glance that said *suspicious.*

"Brittney?" Dixie frowned. "I can see why Warren would make his daughter his beneficiary, but under no circumstances can I see Naomi listing Brittney."

"Um-hmm." B.J. waved her fork. "That raised a red flag with me too. So I asked my friend who told me about it, and he said Warren Keller took out both policies."

"Can he do that?" I asked. "Is that legal? Can a person take out life insurance on someone else? I mean, that just seems like an invitation to murder."

"Anyone can take out a life insurance policy on themselves. So, Warren's policy is fine. However, you can't take out a life insurance policy on someone without their consent. I couldn't take out a policy on any of you. I have to prove that I have an insurable interest." She paused for a moment. "I have to prove that your death would cause me harm in order to have a right to insure your life." She glanced at us. "Does that make sense?"

"So a wife or husband would have a reason to insure each other, right?" Dixie asked.

"Exactly, or a parent has a reason to insure their children. It gets harder when you get further outside of the family, but business partners would have a reason to insure each other because if one died, it could harm the business. It looks like Warren and Naomi got life insurance policies when they were married. Warren was considered the owner of the policies. He paid the premiums. If you're the owner, then you can make whatever changes to the policy you want."

My curiosity was piqued. "What kind of changes?"

"Like changing the beneficiaries. When the policies were first drawn up, he was her beneficiary and vice versa. However, at some point, Warren changed the beneficiary so now it's him and his daughter, Brittney." B.J. raised her fork. "Him, I understand. He's a lawyer and the primary bread winner, but her…" She took a minute to take a bite of her lasagna. "Since I was investigating, I decided to check out Dixon Vannover too."

"Please tell me June Vannover had a million-dollar policy on Dixon?" Monica Jill asked.

B.J. took a few minutes to chew and swallow before saying, "Two million."

"Wow!" Dr. Morgan whistled. "Looks like regardless of how well her art sells, she is going to be a wealthy woman."

Monica Jill made a face as she swallowed the milk Dr. Morgan had encouraged her to drink. "He may be insured for two million dollars, but June may need every penny to cover his debts."

"Yikes!" I said. "Was he in bad shape?"

"I looked into his real estate business, and he borrowed funds from the business to support his political campaign. Plus, there's the big house in that gated community and two expensive cars. Dixon Vannover liked to live well above his means."

"Beau was going to bring this to the meeting, but he checked around, and Dixon Vannover owed a lot of people money," Dixie said. "I don't know if they will all be able to collect, but June will probably need to sell the real estate business and the house."

Dr. Morgan cleared his throat. "Well, I took the scraps from the material found around Naomi Keller's neck to forensics and asked if they could expedite the analysis. Madison was right. It appears to have been a lead used for dog shows."

"I wonder whose lead it was?" I asked.

"Hard to tell at a dog show," Dixie said. "A lot of people who compete in obedience and agility also compete in conformation. So it could have belonged to anyone, including Naomi herself."

"I didn't get Dixon Vannover's body," Dr. Morgan said, "but I called Red and asked him to make sure that they compare the garrote used on Vannover to the one used on Naomi."

Monica Jill's phone rang. "Oh, this is the realtor for that building you sent me." She took the call, but after a few minutes, it was clear from her face and tone that it was bad news. She hung up. "Phooey, that building is sold."

"While we were talking to Brittney Keller at the Greyhound rescue, she happened to mention that they're going to be selling that building," Dixie said.

"It would be perfect because it's already been renovated . . . well, mostly," I said. "There's still going to be some things you're going to want to change."

We talked about the building, and Monica Jill made a few phone calls. It didn't take long for her to locate the listing agent and arrange a formal showing for the next day. She was even more excited when she smiled and said, "Guess what?"

No one even hazarded a guess, but it didn't dampen her enthusiasm. "The building owner is Barbara Westfield." She looked at us expectantly. However, neither of us knew why that name mattered until she said, "Red's sister. She owns the property and is going to be the one showing it to us tomorrow."

"Oh, goody," I said. I'd previously promised to go with Dixie to see the building, and I now wondered if I had time to get a full makeover.

On the ride home, Dixie and I chatted about the baby, the building, and what we'd learned.

"Given the amount of money Warren Keller pulls down, is it surprising that he and Naomi would have million-dollar insurance policies?" Dixie asked.

"Not really. In fact, it's not even unusual that Dixon Vannover has a two-million-dollar policy. He's the primary breadwinner and has all of those business interests." I leaned back on the seat and tried to pull my thoughts into a relevant response. "However, I do believe that those policies give June, Warren, and Brittney a million reasons to commit murder."

Chapter 23

I hadn't heard from Red all day, so I wasn't surprised to see his truck at my house when Dixie brought me home. Dixie was under the misguided impression that Red and I would need some alone time. I pointed out that we would hardly be alone with Stephanie, Joe, Madison, and David. Not to mention Aggie, Rex, Lucky, Turbo, and probably Steve Austin in tow.

We went in, and after dropping off my purse, we immediately followed the noise and went out back, where the humans sat talking and the dogs were playing in the grass.

When we sat down with our adult beverages in hand, the conversation made its way to the murder.

"Dixon Vannover was strangled with something similar to the dog lead that was used on Naomi Keller," Red said, "but we won't know for sure until forensics is done."

"Where was he found?" I asked.

"In their backyard. June found him when she stumbled over the body."

"Ugh. What a horrible thing, to find your spouse dead."

Red's silence spoke volumes.

"What?"

"She claims she didn't talk to him, but one of the neighbors heard them arguing."

"You can't believe June killed him? She was going to leave him. She'd sold some artwork and realizes now that she could be independent. She didn't need to kill him."

The silence that greeted me indicated that I was the only person who believed June was innocent. I turned to Dixie. "You can't believe she did it? You saw how she looked today."

Dixie hung her head.

"What?"

"Lilly Ann, we saw June with a handsome Superman lawyer, and we know she had a two-million-dollar life insurance policy on her husband."

"*What?*" Red shouted.

David laughed. "I think you have some 'splaining to do, Lucy."

I took a few minutes and told everyone about our trip to June Vannover's and also what we'd learned while at Monica Jill's house. "Oh, and Monica Jill is expecting."

Both Stephanie and Madison's faces lit up.

Madison clapped. "Wow! Is she excited?"

I hesitated. "I wouldn't exactly call it excitement. I think she's in shock and has a bit of fear, but I feel confident excitement will be her next emotional stop."

"Well, I had a rather heated day." Madison gave Red a sideways glance and continued after receiving a nod from him. "Naomi Keller and Dixon Vannover exchanged some very steamy e-mails." She fanned herself.

"Really?" Dixie asked. "Anything fit for mixed company?"

"Nothing very original. Naomi's messages were spent stroking Dixon's ego about how amazing he was. How he was a better man and a better lover than her husband. Dixon's messages were about how much he couldn't wait until they could be together all the time. How his wife was just a stupid boat anchor who was dragging him down, but Naomi would be a credit to him and would make a huge splash in Washington."

"That man's opinion of himself was so large, it's a wonder he could tolerate himself," Dixie said. "His ego was bigger than the state of Tennessee."

"It was certainly bigger than his IQ," Stephanie said.

Madison leaned forward. "I know, right? It's the twenty-first century. Why on earth would you put anything in writing you didn't want broadcast all over the news." She glanced at each of us. "I mean, the man was running for political office. His political opponents wouldn't have had to search hard to find out that he was cheating on his wife."

Stephanie sighed. "I'm sorry, Mom. I know you don't want to believe that June killed him, but if she did, I certainly don't blame her."

"Actually, a pretty strong case could be made against her," Red said. "In fact, I'd say the case against June is much stronger than anything against Dixie."

"That makes me feel better . . . I guess," Dixie said.

"What do you mean?" I asked.

"Dixie had motive, means, and opportunity to kill Naomi Keller. They had a history and were seen fighting earlier in the day, but we can't find that Dixie had a reason for murdering Dixon, and considering she was here with two TBI officers while Dixon was murdered, I'd say her alibi is sound."

Dixie looked surprised. "Does this mean I'm off the hook?"

Red smiled. "As far as I'm concerned, you were never on the hook, but I do believe anyone would have a hard time making a case against you stick."

Dixie held up her glass. "I'll drink to that."

"Let's ask our legal expert." Red turned to Stephanie. "What do you think?"

Stephanie thought for a few minutes. "It's been hard to remain objective and not allow my personal feelings to color my judgment in this case, but I honestly think Red's right." She turned to Dixie. "It looks like the two murders are related. Aunt Dixie had no motive and no opportunity to kill Dixon Vannover, so I think she's safe."

"Woohoo!" Dixie cheered, and we all toasted and drank, to Stephanie's assessment.

"I can't wait to tell Beau." Dixie rose. "Thank you, all. I hate to celebrate and run, but I think I'm going to have the first really good night's sleep I've had in nearly a week." She turned to me. "Do you want me to pick you up tomorrow?"

I nodded.

"We'll go take a look at the building and go to the wake, and then it'll be time for your final walk-through." She bid everyone good-bye and then hurried on her way.

Not long after Dixie left, David left to take Madison home. Joe had been unusually quiet, but he asked Stephanie and Lucky if they wanted to go for a ride downtown. So they left, leaving Red and me alone.

"So it looks like I'm going to meet one of your sisters tomorrow."

"Which one?"

"Barbara." I explained about the doggie day care and the possibility that Dixie might buy the building. "I wish I had the time to get my hair and nails done."

He chuckled. "You look beautiful, and I'm sure Barbara will love you as much as I do."

I smiled. "I doubt that. You're her baby brother, and I'm sure no woman will be good enough for you in the eyes of your mother and sisters."

He took my hand. "Stop it. I'm the one who's lucky." He leaned over and kissed me. "I'm not one of those romantic men who will walk around spouting poetry, and I'm not going to open my chest and start baring my soul. I'm pretty basic." He paused. "Even before the war, I wasn't someone who talked about their feelings, but that doesn't mean I don't care."

"I know." I reached out a hand and ran it along the scar on the side of his face. "I know you went through a lot that you don't want to talk about or relive, but one day I hope you will feel like you can trust me enough to share the burden of those memories."

"I trust you with my life . . . and my heart, but there are things that no one should have to endure. There are evil people in this world. Not just bad or mean, but pure evil. I don't talk about what happened when I was a POW and tortured, because there are demons I'm not ready to face yet."

"When you are, I'm here."

We kissed until Aggie hopped up on my lap and wiggled her way in between us.

"If I didn't know better, I'd say Aggie was jealous of the attention you were giving me."

I laughed. "She definitely needs to be the center of attention."

Red stood up. "I better go."

I walked him to the door and spent more time saying good night. When he finally left, I felt breathless, and my heart was racing.

Experience told me that regardless of the amount of time they'd spent outside, Rex and Aggie would need a formal potty break before bed. So I let them outside one last time, and they quickly took care of business.

Inside, I let the poodles get into bed, while I took a shower and got ready for sleep. When I was done, I spent some time checking my e-mails. I had one from the agent at my mortgage company saying that, as far as she was concerned, I was good to go for my Friday closing. Before putting away my laptop, I logged into my bank to review the instructions for requesting a wire transfer so I would be set to initiate that tomorrow.

Once I had signed in to my account, I was shocked when I looked at my balance. There was more money than I expected. Significantly more. Reviewing the transaction history, I saw that a large deposit was made just two days ago. The information available online was brief and cryptic. I would need to find out where the money came from and why it was in my account.

Chapter 24

Early Thursday morning, I got up and went through my morning routine. By the time David and Stephanie joined me on the back deck for coffee, I had been awake for a couple of hours.

David stumbled into his chair, careful not to spill his coffee as he flopped down. He downed a few ounces before attempting to talk. "Aren't you off today? Why are you dressed so early?"

"I am off from work, but I'm going to meet Dixie to check out a building. We're going to Naomi Keller's visitation, and then I have the final inspection, plus I still have to wire the money to the title company and—"

David held up his hand. "You're making my head spin. Sounds like you've got a busy day."

"And I'm going to meet one of Red's sisters. So I've been up most of the night stressing about that."

David smiled as he sipped his coffee. "I think meeting Red's family is merely a formality. He really cares about you. I'm sure they will too."

"What if they don't?"

"Red's a grown man. He's capable of making his own decisions. He isn't going to break up with you simply because his sisters don't like you."

"I know, but I know what it's like to be . . . involved with someone whose family doesn't like you."

Stephanie had been quiet up until now. "You're thinking about Nonna Conti."

Nonna Conti was Albert's mother. She'd hated me from the moment I'd married her son. I tried never to speak ill of her, especially in front of David and Stephanie. Regardless of my feelings, she was still their *nonna*, their grandmother. However, Camilia Conti had no qualms about speaking ill of me in their presence. I couldn't say that her feelings had played a factor in the dissolution of our marriage, but it had certainly added stress.

Stephanie reached out a hand of comfort, and it was then that I noticed the large diamond that now graced her ring finger.

"*Oh my god! You're engaged!*" I grabbed her face and stared into her eyes. The happiness that greeted me let me know all that I needed to know. My daughter was engaged, and she was happy. We hugged and cried and hugged while we cried, and then we laughed and cried.

David was a bit slower to respond, but he eventually reached over and gave Stephanie a hug. "I'm really happy for you, sis. Joe's a good man."

Stephanie cried some more, and Lucky, unsure what to make of all of this, stood by ready to provide comfort if needed.

Stephanie reached down and hugged her dog. "It's okay, boy. These are tears of joy."

"I'm assuming all of this happened last night, but how did he propose? Had you two talked about it?"

Stephanie sat up. "Last night, he took me down by the Tennessee River. There's a place near the water with a bench. We sat and watched the water. Then he got down on one knee. He told me he loved me and wanted to spend the rest of his life with me. He said if that meant he had to move to Chicago, then so be it. He asked if I'd marry him."

"How romantic." I started to tear up again and had to wipe my eyes.

"I didn't even think twice. I just knew that I wanted to marry him, and I said yes."

"I don't suppose you've had time to think about a date yet?"

"Not yet. We have some important details to work through first."

"Like who quits their job and moves?" David said.

Something in David's voice made me wonder if that question was strictly for Stephanie and Joe or if he was thinking similar thoughts about him and Madison, but I decided to let that question wait.

The alarm on my cell phone went off, and I remembered that I needed to call the bank. So I quickly dialed that number. Despite the fact that the branch had just opened, I was still placed in a queue. Thankfully, my wait was brief. I asked about the deposit, and the teller confirmed the conclusion I'd come to in the early hours of the morning. I arranged for the wire transfer and hung up.

"I don't think I've ever heard anyone question their bank because they have too much money," David said.

"Apparently, the police and the courts have finished investigating your father. Remember the million dollars he had in that offshore bank?

Well, they've released the money to me." I stared at them. "I don't want the money, and I'm thinking I'd like to set up trusts for the two of you."

Stephanie and David exchanged glances.

"What's wrong? I expected you two would be at least a little excited." I turned to Stephanie. "You and Joe can use the money to have the wedding of your dreams or use it for a down payment on a new house. Honeymoon in Italy. Or you can use it as a nest egg for my future grandchildren's college funds."

Stephanie rolled her eyes. "Can you really imagine Joe Harrison wearing a tuxedo in some big fancy wedding?" She glanced out over the yard. "I love him too much to ask that of him. I'd be content to get married here, in your gazebo surrounded by my family."

I fought back tears.

Stephanie grinned. "Maybe you and Red will want to throw a big elaborate wedding."

I laughed. "I have an easier time imagining Joe in a tux than imagining Red wearing one."

I turned to David. "Well, what about you? New York is an expensive place to live, and you could get a bigger, nicer apartment or travel the world."

David glanced at Stephanie and then cleared his throat. "We both talked about this, and we decided that rather than splitting the money two ways, we want to split it three ways." He pointed to all of us. I started to object, but he hurried on. "Mom, you've sacrificed so much for us over the years, and you're always putting others first. It's time that you . . . lived a little. You could pay cash for this house. Renovate it however you want. Travel the world."

Stephanie gazed at me. "Isn't there something you've always dreamed of doing, but never had the money?"

I thought for a few moments. "Well, there's one thing."

Both of them sat up and leaned forward eagerly.

"Yesterday, when I was walking around that building with Dixie, I thought it might be nice to be a partner or an investor."

Stephanie bounced in her chair. "I think that's a great idea. You could take care of the accounting for the business."

I glanced at David. "What do you think, and be honest, I can take it."

"I think it's a great idea, too. You won't need anything as fancy as that Pet Haven Spa where Madison used to work, but I'm sure she'd want to help out too."

We chatted about the business until Dixie arrived. I cautioned the children that nothing was confirmed yet. We were just *looking* at the building, and even if Dixie decided to move forward, I wasn't sure she'd want a partner.

On the drive downtown, I thought of how to broach the subject with Dixie but never found a good opening. Before I realized it, we were at the Greyhound rescue. Monica Jill called and said she was going to be late and for us to go ahead without her.

We parked in the same spot we had the previous night. The rescue wasn't open yet, but there was a black luxury SUV parked in front. A woman with thick, curly dark hair and a big smile greeted us. She wore blue jeans and a top I'd seen in one of my favorite shops, which I loved, though I knew it was outside of my price range. She introduced herself.

"Hello, I'm Barbara Westfield."

Dixie shook her hand. "I'm Scarlet Jefferson, but please call me Dixie." She turned to me. "This is my best friend in the entire world, Lilly Ann Echosby."

I saw the name recognition reflected in her eyes. "Lilly Ann Echosby? Are you... I mean, you're the Lilly Echosby who's dating my brother, Red?"

I nodded and extended my hand.

Barbara Westfield ignored my hand, reached out, and pulled me into a warm hug. "I can't believe I'm finally getting to meet you." She released me and smiled. "I had no idea you were coming too. My sisters are going to be so jealous when I tell them I got to meet you." She smiled and leaned forward and whispered, "My brother is crazy about you."

I laughed. "Well, I'm pretty crazy about him too."

She reached out and hugged me again. "I'm sorry, but I'm a hugger, and I just can't tell you how excited we are." She released me. "Okay, I'll try not to do that again."

"It's okay." I chuckled. "I've been nervous about meeting Red's family, so it'll be nice to know that I have a friend."

She stopped and put her hand on her hip. "Nervous? Honey, you have no reason to be nervous. We are thrilled." She stared a few moments longer and then remembered why we were all here. "I'm sorry. Let me get the door open. I can show you around, and then we can chat more."

Barbara showed us the building and pointed out every feature, both good and bad. She kept up a steady string of conversation the entire time, and when we'd seen everything, she returned us to the office space. By that time, Monica Jill had arrived, and she sat in the office and waited.

Monica Jill was excited to meet Barbara Westfield, but she wasn't her normally bubbly self and didn't say much.

Barbara looked at us and then down at her jeans. "You three look really nice. I feel like I should have dressed up."

"We're going to a wake later," Dixie said.

"I'm sorry. It wouldn't be for Naomi Keller, would it?"

We nodded.

Barbara didn't say a word, but I could feel the temperature decrease.

"Did you know Naomi Keller?" I asked.

"Not well, but I'd had some . . . dealings with her."

"Sounds like you didn't like her," Monica Jill said.

She hesitated for a few moments. "I don't like to speak ill of the dead, but Naomi Keller was a . . . difficult woman."

"How so?" I asked. "And, before you get your guard up, I think you should know that we weren't friends with Naomi Keller."

Barbara glanced at each of us. "None of you were?"

"Good Lord, no," Monica Jill said.

"Well, why are you going to the visitation?"

"Because the police think I might have killed her," Dixie said, "and we're hoping to find the real killer so we can get them off my back."

Barbara's face showed that she hadn't expected that response. After a moment of shocked surprise, she said, "Wow! They really think you killed her?"

"Your brother is helping us, but he took me in for questioning."

She put her hand on her hip again. "No way. Well, you just tell him there's probably a long line of people who would have liked to have killed Naomi Keller."

Something in her face made me ask, "I don't suppose you know any of those people?"

She thought for a few moments before making up her mind. "Well, Brittney Keller would be at the top of my list, if I had to name someone."

"Why's that?" Monica Jill asked.

"For some reason I'll never understand, Brittney was head over heels for Dixon Vannover. She was devastated when he dropped her like a bad habit about two months ago. You should have heard the wailing and cursing she did." Barbara shook her head at the thought. "I told her she was better off without that loser, but she wouldn't hear anything against him." She clutched her chest. "She was in love."

"So Brittney talked about the fact that her lover and her stepmother were . . . an item?" I asked.

"Frankly, I'd have taken that to my grave, but she told anyone dumb enough to stand still and listen. I made the mistake of coming to have a look around the building, and she trapped me, and I heard about the whole sordid mess."

"You know she came to the dog show the day Naomi Keller was killed and staged a protest in which she actually flung syrup on her stepmother," Monica Jill said.

"I told her she should have flung that syrup at Dixon Vannover." Barbara folded her arms across her chest. "That two-timing womanizer had the nerve to try and get her back after Naomi was dead."

"What?" we all said.

"Oh yeah, he came here the other night and practically begged her to forgive him and take him back. I had come to take pictures of the building. Well, I guess she finally either got fed up or saw him for the lowlife that he is . . . was, because she called him every name in the book. She screamed some obscenities that made me blush, and I spend a good amount of time around construction workers."

"When was this fight?" I asked.

"I think it was Tuesday night." She thought. "It was Tuesday, because that's the night he died, and I remember telling my husband that Brittney had been mad enough to kill."

We asked a few more questions, but Barbara didn't have any other information about Naomi Keller or Dixon Vannover. Eventually, our attention returned to the building.

"I don't know how you feel about this office area, but I absolutely hate it. I wanted to open it up, but the Greyhound rescue didn't have the money for more renovations, and my husband had already discounted their rent so much that he positively refused to do anything else."

"So you and your husband own the building and leased the space to the rescue?" Dixie asked.

"We bought up a lot of these old buildings. Since he's a contractor, he can renovate them and either sell them or lease them. He wasn't crazy about making these customized changes because he said we'd never get our money back from a nonprofit and it would just make the building harder to sell." She smiled. "I hope you decide to buy this place, if for no other reason than it will allow me to rub his nose in it."

Dixie said she needed to think about it, so we prepared to go. Barbara Westfield said her good-byes to Monica Jill and Dixie. She hugged me again and whispered, "Thank you."

"For what?"

"You've made my brother so happy. He's almost back to the way he was before he went . . . before the military." She choked up. "I don't know if he'll ever get back completely, but he's interested in life again, and he laughs and plays with that goofy dog. It's just wonderful."

I could feel the heat rise up my neck, and I reached out and hugged Barbara. "Thank you."

Monica Jill, Dixie, and I arranged to meet at Da Vinci's to discuss our next steps.

Dixie and I arrived first and found a small bistro table outside, and over coffee and croissants, we talked through the building's pluses and minuses. We waited for Monica Jill, who got stuck in traffic and then took a bathroom break.

When Monica Jill finally sat down, I leaned forward and asked the question that had been eating at me. "What did your husband say about the baby?"

Monica Jill sighed. "I didn't tell him."

"*What?*"

"Zach was tired and cranky when he came home last night, and I just couldn't do it." She must have seen that we were both revved up to protest because she held up her hand. "However, I told him that I had something I wanted to talk to him about tonight, and I'm planning a romantic dinner and some quiet time for us to talk. I'll tell him tonight."

She seemed much more at ease with the news than she had yesterday, which would certainly be a huge help when she talked with her husband. We spent a few minutes talking about the baby but then moved on to the matter at hand.

"So what did you think of the building?" Monica Jill asked.

"I loved just about everything about it." Dixie said. "Unfortunately, the one thing I don't love is the biggest obstacle—the price."

"Well, we might be able to get her to come down a bit," Monica Jill said, without the slightest bit of conviction in her voice. "But I do think the price is fair."

"So do I," Dixie said. "That's the problem. Beau and I talked about it last night. He's willing to do whatever I want." She smiled but then shook her head. "But I hate to ask him to invest so much money. He's been slowing down and talking about retiring in a few years. This would delay his plan."

"Maybe we can find another building, but I doubt that we'll find one that is as close to what you want. The location is amazing, but God will provide." Monica Jill bit into her croissant.

While Dixie munched on her flakey, buttery croissant, I screwed up my courage. "I talked to the kids this morning, and we were wondering if you would consider taking on a partner."

I quickly explained about Albert's legacy and how I would love to invest in the day care. "I could help with the books, and I wouldn't have to be involved in the day-to-day operations," I quickly added. "Unless you wanted me to. It would be your business. I could be a silent partner or an investor."

Dixie burst into tears and then reached over and hugged me. "Lilly Ann, that's the most wonderful thing I've ever heard. I would love to have you as a full partner." She pulled back to look at my face. "If you're sure that's what you want?"

"I'm sure."

Monica Jill clapped. "Oh my God! That is fantastic."

We pulled ourselves together and talked through what we felt would be a fair price to offer for the building, and Monica Jill pulled out her phone. "Technically, I'll have to get someone from the office to help with the sale. I'm not licensed for commercial real estate, but I can call Barbara and let her know we're interested in making an offer." She crossed her fingers. "Maybe if she knows her brother's girlfriend is going to be an investor in the business, she might just hold off on other offers until we can get a formal sales contract worked out."

Before I could object to using my relationship with Red to help in the business deal, Monica Jill dialed Barbara Westfield and told her that her buyer was interested in making an offer. Based on Monica Jill's animated facial expressions, it looked like Barbara Westfield was willing to consider an offer.

We sat and discussed our offer amount and the items we wanted added into the contract until it was time to leave for Naomi Keller's visitation. The funeral home was atop Lookout Mountain, so I endured another perilous ascent that left my stomach in knots.

As I climbed out of Dixie's car, she looked at my drawn expression. "I would have thought you'd find it easier to get up and down the mountain by now."

"So would I."

A visitation, or wake, was an opportunity for individuals to come and say their good-byes to the deceased and to offer condolences to the family. I've been to some wakes that were more like a party than a sad acknowledgment of a death. However, it wasn't uncommon for a wake to function like an open house, where people dropped in, signed the guest book, viewed the body, and left.

Monica Jill arrived atop the mountain not long after us, but we could see she was on the telephone, and she motioned for us to go ahead. We walked into the funeral home, expecting to see a crowd of people milling around, but instead found ourselves alone.

I looked at my watch. "Do you think we got the time wrong?"

"Nope. You're right on time." Brittney Keller had sneaked up behind us while we were focused on signing the guest book. "This turnout speaks volumes about Naomi's popularity, don't you think?"

Brittney was dressed in a bright red cocktail dress, which was lowcut and daring, with high stiletto shoes. Before I could control my face, she twirled. "You don't like my outfit?" She laughed and leaned close. "I intend to dance on that hag's grave, so I needed something appropriate for the occasion."

"If you're only here to disgrace yourself, why'd you even bother coming?" Dixie said.

"I came for Daddy. It's the only way he would agree to pay my cut of the stepmonster's insurance money."

"You know about that?" I asked.

"I didn't, until yesterday. When I refused to come to this farce, Daddy Dearest dangled an amount of money large enough to fund my move to Florida in front of my nose. So . . . here I am."

"Where's your father?" Dixie asked.

Brittney strutted to one of the rooms in the funeral home and flung open the door. We followed her and saw a room set up with chairs for anyone wishing to linger and a huge picture of Naomi Keller in her younger days, which looked as though she were made up for a Glamour Shot photo, resting on an easel near the front of the room.

Before Brittney could march off, I grabbed her arm. "Where's the body?"

"The police haven't released it yet, but my father plans to have her cremated anyway, so there was no reason to wait."

Dixie and I walked to the front of the room to give our condolences to Warren Keller, the lone person in a room full of empty chairs.

I extended my hand and mumbled something that I thought sounded appropriate for the occasion. After all, I barely knew the woman and wasn't great at spewing out sentiment in any case. However, Dixie was highly skilled.

She hugged him. "I'm so sorry for your loss."

"Thank you. Thank you both for coming." He looked from me to Dixie. "I hear from Brittney that you two have been asking a lot of questions about Naomi's death."

I wasn't sure how to respond, but Dixie stepped in. "Well, I can't help feeling partly responsible. If she hadn't been judging our event . . . who knows?"

He reached out and squeezed each of our arms. "That's so kind. I truly appreciate you both for risking the wrath of a murderer to find who killed her." He glanced around. "Naomi didn't have a lot of friends, so I'm glad she had you both."

I felt a warm flush rising up my neck at the deception. Neither Dixie nor I were friends of Naomi Keller. In fact, if Dixie hadn't been accused of the murder, I seriously doubt that we'd have thought twice about it, which made me sad. Regardless of how rotten of a human being she was, the idea that hardly anyone would grieve her death seemed extremely cruel. My guilt prompted me. "If there is anything you need, please don't hesitate to ask."

Warren Keller teared up. "Well, there is one thing."

I grimaced, but Dixie picked up the baton of goodwill. "Certainly, just name it."

"I'd like to donate Naomi's clothes to charity." He glanced at Dixie. "I think you're involved in a lot of charitable organizations that help women in the community, and I thought . . ."

"I'm on the board of an organization that helps homeless women find jobs. Many of them don't have the proper wardrobe, and I'm sure they'd be glad to have Naomi's things, but . . ." She glanced at Brittney.

"Saying Brittney and her stepmother didn't get along is like saying oil and water don't mix." He pointed to his daughter. "She'd just burn everything."

We worked out a date and time that would work for the three of us, and then Dixie and I moved along. By now, our friends and family had arrived and provided a respectable number of visitors, which I was sure had to make Warren Keller feel a bit better.

They each came up and shook Warren's hands and offered words of condolence.

Brittney sat on the front row reading a magazine and chewing bubblegum.

We milled around for a bit, but after a decent interval of time, we rose and prepared to make our exit.

I walked over to Red. "Will I see you tonight?"

"If that's an invite, then *yes*."

"Absolutely."

His eyes asked a question I wasn't picking up on. Eventually, he said, "So how did the meeting with Barbara go?"

I smiled. "She's so nice. I love her."

"I knew you didn't have anything to worry about. I hope she didn't say anything to embarrass me."

I gave him a knowing smile, which I knew would raise his anxiety.

"Wait, what did she say?"

I laughed. "Nothing. She was just very nice."

At first, he didn't look as though he believed me, but after a few minutes, he shook his head. "Forget it. It's probably going to be worse for me at the housewarming when they're all there together. My mom and my sisters will love embarrassing me. I just hope no one starts pulling out old baby pictures."

"I'd love to see your baby pictures." I kissed him. "Do you have time to join us for lunch?"

He looked at his watch. "No, I've got a lot of work, but I'll see you tonight."

Rather than having me face the harrowing trip down the mountain so quickly after our ascent, Dixie thought it would be nice to have lunch at a restaurant. She suggested a café that had been a grocery store in a previous life but was now a lovely restaurant with a large patio area.

Red and Madison were unable to join us, but our party of eight was accommodated by pushing three tables together.

The food was good Southern cuisine with a gourmet touch and included items like fried green tomatoes, pimiento cheese, and shrimp and grits. Since we were split fifty-fifty between North and South, we decided to order a variety of dishes and share them. When our plates arrived, everything looked, smelled, and tasted wonderful.

When we were full, we sat back and sipped our sweet tea and made sure that everyone was up to date on the latest.

"I'm sure you'll all hear from Red later, but the forensic report came back from the fabric used to garrote both Naomi Keller and Dixon Vannover," Dr. Morgan said. "Madison was correct. It was a dog lead, but that's not the most interesting thing." He took a sip of his tea. "The interesting fact was that a small hair was found on the lead."

"Oh my," Monica Jill said. "Were they able to run DNA and trace the hair to the killer?" She reached over and grabbed a fried potato from B.J.'s plate. "Are you going to eat these?"

B.J. slid her plate toward her friend. "I saw that on one of those forensic shows, and they were able to find the killer from a hair he left at the scene of the crime."

"It turns out this hair wasn't human."

"Not human? What kind of hair was it?" Dixie asked.

"Animal hair."

"Well, that's no surprise," Dixie said. "I mean, she was killed at a dog show, and there were lots of dogs there. Plus she owns Greyhounds. There must be dog hair everywhere."

"True, but it wasn't canine hair. It was feline."

B.J. shrugged. "A lot of people have both cats and dogs."

Joe said, "Were they able to run any DNA tests to trace the hair?"

"Trace the hair?" Dr. Morgan asked. "They can do that?"

"Oh my God," Stephanie said, sitting up. "Last year, I met this prosecutor from Prince Edward Island. We were talking about unusual cases, and he mentioned a case where the prosecutors used cat hairs found on a bloodied jacket to link a man to the murder of his estranged wife."

Dr. Morgan, Stephanie, and Joe entered into a detailed and extremely confusing conversation about DNA, animal hair, and trace evidence. After a few moments, Stephanie glanced at the rest of us. "I'm sorry."

"Does Chattanooga have the equipment to do whatever it is you've all been discussing?" I asked.

"I'm not sure, but I can ask," Dr. Morgan said. "In fact, I'm going to check into this right now." He got up, left money for the bill, and then hurried out to his car.

Dixie frowned.

"What's wrong?" I asked.

"I'm just wondering which one of our suspects had a cat."

"I saw a cat in June Vannover's artist shed. She said Dixon was allergic, so the cat had to stay in the shed."

"There was a cat in the Greyhound rescue," Monica Jill reminded us.

Dixie glanced at me. "I didn't see one at Warren Keller's house when we were there, did you?"

"Neither did I, but . . ." Something tugged at my memory. An idea. A thought or memory flitted across my brain. I tried to catch it, but it was gone too quickly. After a few moments, I shook it off. Whatever it was, it was gone now. My gut told me it was important, but experience told me to push it away and stop trying. At some point, it would come to me. However, something in the pit of my stomach sent a shiver down my spine, and I shuddered. Whatever it was that was lurking just outside of my conscience mind was important. I just prayed that whenever I caught it, it wouldn't be too late.

Chapter 25

I glanced at my watch. "I need to get back. I've got a final inspection in less than an hour."

We paid for our meals and then made our way down the mountain.

The inspector was waiting in the driveway when we got there. He'd already inspected once, so this visit was merely verifying that the few repairs the bank requested had been completed. In record time, the inspection was over, and I was cleared for closing the next day.

David and Madison were going to dinner and then a play at the Tivoli Theatre in downtown Chattanooga. He showered, dressed, and then hurried off. Stephanie and Joe also had plans, so she dressed, and then they headed out for dinner on the riverboat, leaving Turbo and Lucky to play in the yard with Aggie and Rex. When Red arrived with Steve Austin, it was a rousing good time of rough-and-tumble play, with several rounds of Catch Me If You Can. Red and I sat on the back deck and watched the dogs racing around the yard with a zeal and enthusiasm that brought a smile to my face.

Red cooked penne pasta and sausage in a red sauce that was spicy and delicious. I made a chopped salad and opened a bottle of wine.

I shared Dr. Morgan's revelation about the animal hair found on the lead used to kill Naomi Keller. Red had already read the forensic report, but he was excited to learn that they might be able to trace the hair to a specific cat.

"I'm curious how they can pull that off," he said. "We have to run human DNA through a database and hope to find a match. I guess if we could get DNA from the cats of our suspects, we may be able to narrow things down, but . . . I can't imagine it'll be admissible in court."

"Stephanie said a prosecutor did it in Canada, but . . . I have no idea."

We talked about cats, dogs, and the wonders of modern science. Then I told him about our visit to the building and the possibility that I would invest in the doggie day care with Dixie. I watched his face carefully. "What do you think?"

"I think if that's what you want, then you should do it."

"I mean, do you think it's a good investment?"

He smiled. "I didn't know much about dogs before I met you and Dixie and your crazy dog club friends, but now . . ." He glanced across the yard at Steve Austin, who had just taken a stuffed toy from Lucky and was running around the yard with a look of pure joy on his face. "Now I realize there are a lot of dog owners out there who love their animals. I also know there are a lot of energetic dogs that need exercise." He pointed at Steve Austin. "Normally, when I come home from work, he's so excited that he just wants to play for hours, but I'm exhausted by then, and I just want a nap. When he comes here and plays or when he can play with Turbo, he's worn out, and when I get home, he's content to just snuggle up on my lap and watch television." He glanced at me. "Are you having second thoughts?"

I shook my head. "Not at all. I'm just . . . I don't know, nervous. I feel . . . a little frightened."

"About the money?"

"No. I'm just so happy. I mean, I have Aggie and Rex. My friends, the dog club, and my new job. Tomorrow, I close on this house, and . . . I have you." I smiled.

He leaned over and kissed me. "Your happy place?"

I nodded. "I guess I'm afraid something will go wrong."

"Well, I can't guarantee that nothing will go wrong, but I can promise you that whatever happens, I'll be here."

The next day, I was nervous, but my early-morning closing went by without a hitch. The title company received the funds, and I signed my name until I got a cramp in my hand. I was so excited to have Stephanie and David there, and when I was handed the keys, they hugged and celebrated with me.

Since I had been renting the house, I didn't expect to be as emotional as I was, but there is something very permanent about buying and owning your own home.

We spent the rest of the day picking up decorations, food, and supplies for the housewarming. Unfortunately, Red had to work late and wasn't able to join us for dinner, so I was able to enjoy a little quiet time with my children at the end of the day.

It was another lovely summer evening, so we ate outside and reviewed our decorating handywork.

"I think everything looks great." Stephanie scanned the flowers we'd spent the afternoon planting to brighten up the yard.

David mowed and edged the grass, and Stephanie and I filled planters with annuals, which we used to line the edge of the deck.

"I love your yard," Stephanie said. "I was only half joking about getting married here."

I squeezed her hand. "I'd love that. What does Joe want?"

She smiled. "Whatever makes me happy."

"What will make you happy?"

She thought for a minute. "Actually, being closer to family." She smiled. "We're talking about possibly relocating to Chattanooga."

I gasped. "Do you mean it?" My eyes filled with tears. "I would love that so much." I hugged my daughter.

"Red thinks he could get Joe a job at TBI. I'd have to pass the bar in Tennessee to be able to practice here, but I love the weather, and if we start a family one day, then I'd want to be closer to you."

I hugged her again. "Oh, my goodness. That's just the most amazing . . ." I choked up. When I was able to talk, I turned to David. "What about you?"

"I'm not ready to give up my career and move to Tennessee . . . not yet anyway. Madison and I are still feeling each other out and testing the waters. I'm hoping she'll come to New York for a visit." He shrugged. "Who knows? She may like it; she may not. But if both of you are here, then I will definitely have a lot more reasons to come for a visit."

"You are always welcome."

We spent a long time sitting out and talking about the future. When I eventually went to bed, I spent a long time thinking about my life and how incredibly blessed I was. I thanked God for the direction my life had taken and for everything that had led me to Chattanooga and this place.

Aggie slept next to me and gave a short woof. I glanced at my sleeping dog and couldn't help wondering if she was dreaming about playing Catch Me If You Can in her sleep. After a few minutes, I reminded myself that tomorrow I needed to get up early to go with Dixie to pack up Naomi Keller's clothes to donate to the homeless shelter. I tried not to dwell on the contrast between the path that Naomi Keller's life had taken and my own. She must have been extremely unhappy in her marriage. Warren Keller was a hard man, who was, if the rumors were to be believed, very controlling. I wondered if she'd loved Dixon Vannover. He too had been controlling of his wife. Had June gotten tired of his philandering and murdered him?

She had a motive. She had the opportunity to kill both Naomi and Dixon. June Vannover didn't have a dog. She could have killed Naomi Keller at the dog club and used one of Naomi's leads, but would she have taken an extra lead to finish off her husband?

Brittney Keller also had a good reason to kill both Dixon and Naomi. Red's sister heard her arguing with him. She openly admitted that she hated her stepmother. She was at the dog club when Naomi was murdered, and she had access to the lead that was used to garrote both her cheating boyfriend and her stepmother, whom he'd cheated with. She had motive. She had the opportunity, and she had the means. She would now get the money from her stepmother's insurance policy. Plus she had a cat.

My muscles ached from the yard work and planting, and I struggled to think. I was missing something important, but for the life of me, I couldn't remember it. I hoped whatever the missing piece to this puzzle was, I'd remember it when I needed to. I just hoped that need would come quickly.

Chapter 26

I was awakened by a weight on my chest. For a brief instant while I was between sleep and conscious thought, I had a moment of panic. Is this what a heart attack feels like? That was until the weight started to use my body as a ramp and walk up and down. I rolled over and dislodged the interloper, hoping she'd go back to sleep, but it was not to be. This time, she walked up to my face and scratched with her paws until she pulled down the covers. When I opened my eyes, I found myself staring into a cold, wet, black nose. Aggie was persistent if nothing else.

I checked the time and then decided those extra forty-five minutes wouldn't make much difference anyway. So I canceled my alarm and scooped up the poodles. I opened Stephanie's door and called Lucky and then took all three dogs outside.

It looked like the weatherman might be right, and today promised to be perfect for an outdoor function. I waited while the dogs took care of their business and then let them back inside and got myself ready for the day. I dressed in a sundress, which I got at an end-of-season sale from the clearance rack at one of the most expensive stores in town. It was my favorite summer dress, and it fit well, which always boosted my confidence.

Dixie picked me up at the designated time. Initially, I planned to leave the dogs at home, but when Dixie arrived in her RV with Chyna and Leia in tow, I decided Aggie, Rex, and Lucky deserved a little time hanging out with their friends. I left a note for the kids, and we set off for yet another mountain trek. I kept my eyes closed for most of the trip. When I felt the car level out, I opened my eyes.

"Sweet mother of God, how do you manage driving this thing up this mountain?"

"I've done it so often I don't even think about it."

"How long do you think this will take?" I asked. "There's still plenty of things to do before everyone arrives this afternoon, and I have at least three more hours of stressing out ahead of me."

"Hopefully, he will have sorted through things and at least gotten boxes for us, but if it takes more than an hour, we'll just tell him we need to come back another time."

Warren Keller opened the door and invited us inside. "You ladies are punctual. I made coffee, and I picked up croissants too."

"We don't really have much time. Lilly Ann has a housewarming in a few hours, and we have a lot of work to do, so we'll take a rain check and just get busy sorting Naomi's things."

His eyes flashed for a moment, but that moment was over quickly. He smiled. "Surely, you have time for coffee."

Not wanting to be rude, Dixie and I accepted the coffee but declined his offer of croissants.

I took a small sip of coffee, afraid I'd spill something on my dress. When he stepped out of the room for a moment, I dumped most of my coffee down the sink. When he returned, he seemed pleased and escorted us to the master bedroom.

A room that had probably at one time been a small nursery, just off the master, had been renovated into a closet for Naomi. The room was outfitted with floor-to-ceiling mahogany cabinets.

Naomi Keller had expensive taste, and her clothes reflected that. Every shirt, pair of pants, and shoe had a designer's name on it somewhere. One entire wall was dedicated to shoes. I recognized names like Jimmy Choo, Louboutin, and Stuart Weitzman. I tried to count how many there were but stopped at a hundred and fifteen.

When Warren left to find us some boxes, I turned to Dixie and said, "Are you seriously going to take those two-thousand-dollar Jimmy Choo boots to the homeless shelter?"

Dixie smiled. "Of course. We won't be able to give them to any of the women because it might make them a target. However, we've been looking for a good fund-raiser, and I think auctioning off Naomi Keller's shoes, furs, and expensive gowns would bring in a lot of money."

"That's a great idea."

She yawned. "We can donate the blue jeans and casual clothes to the clothing pantry, but the more expensive items will be able to benefit more women if we can sell them and use the money for paying for night school or for helping with rent, utility payments, and groceries."

We worked quickly, boxing as many items as we could, but there was no way we would get everything boxed up today.

Dixie yawned for the third or fourth time. "I can't understand why I'm so sleepy."

"I stayed up late thinking about who could possibly have killed Naomi Keller and Dixon Vannover." I glanced around to make sure Warren Keller wasn't nearby. I didn't see him but lowered my voice anyway. "I don't think it was June."

"You don't want it to be June." Dixie yawned. "She had a good motive, and she has a cat."

"I know, but I just don't think she would have taken Naomi Keller's lead and strangled her. I think she would have shot her first."

"I suppose. June is pretty small. Strangling someone takes a lot of strength, doesn't it?"

"If we use that logic, then that would eliminate Brittney too." I shook my head. "But both of them have cats, and Warren—"

That's when it hit me. What I'd been struggling to remember was the cat I'd seen in Warren Keller's backyard the first time we arrived. Just then, the door opened, and Warren Keller stood in the doorway, holding the cat.

"Uh, I didn't know you had a cat."

He smirked. "Now what difference could it make whether I have a cat or not?"

I glanced at Dixie, who seemed to be ready to fall over.

"Oh, your friend is probably going to be asleep in a few minutes," Warren Keller said. "She won't be able to help you." He put the cat down and revealed that, behind, it he had a gun "It would have been a lot less painful if you had drunk your coffee."

I grabbed Dixie's hand and gave it a squeeze. "What did you drug her with?"

"Diazepam. I had planned to use it on Naomi, but I never got a chance."

My brain raced around furiously. *Keep him talking.* I needed to keep him talking. "Why? Why did you kill your wife?"

"Because she was a dirty little tramp. I see women like her every day. They marry a man and promise to love, honor, and obey until death do they part. However, they don't. The first time there's trouble or they see some other poor fool they think can give them more shoes or more jewels, they want to be free." He sneered. "Naomi was just like them. She would drop her skirt for any Tom, Dick, or Dixon who gave her the time of day." He spat on the floor. "She sickened me."

I hadn't noticed the crazy streak in his eyes until that moment. I needed to find a way to get Dixie and me out of that closet, but the only weapon I had to fight with was the pair of Jimmy Choo boots that I had in my hand.

I needed to keep him talking to buy time to figure out how to get us out of this mess. "Why did you kill Dixon Vannover?"

"Vannover was just as bad as Naomi. I had no idea he was having an affair with both my wife *and* my daughter until you two told me when you came with the casserole. He deserved what he got."

Dixie swayed, and I reached out to support my friend before she collapsed. "People know where we are. I left a note."

"You two are going to have an accident." He took a step backward and used the gun to motion for me to come out. "Now, move."

I wrapped my arms around Dixie's waist to support her, and we walked out of the closet and made our way through the house. When I got to the front door, I stopped.

"Go."

I leaned Dixie against my body so I could grab the knob. Once I got the door open, I helped her outside. Dixie was mostly dead weight, and it was a struggle to keep her upright and still move. The Kellers' mountain home was fairly secluded, but he moved the gun to my back so it wouldn't be easily visible to a casual observer.

We walked slowly, propelling Dixie forward as we went. When we got to Dixie's RV, I could hear the poodles barking.

He held the gun to the back of Dixie's head. "Tell them to settle down, or I blow your friend's brains out here and now."

"Quiet." I opened the door to the RV.

Surprisingly, Lucky, Chyna, and Leia obeyed. They weren't my dogs, and I never gave them orders. Aggie and Rex were a different matter. They continued to bark, but their yaps weren't the least bit menacing.

Warren Keller looked irritated, and I could tell he was about to order me again to silence the dogs when Aggie lunged forward and took a flying leap at Warren Keller's face.

Surprised by her assault, Warren Keller tripped on the RV steps and fell onto the ground. Chyna, Leia, and Lucky took that as their cue to attack and bounded out of the RV. The dogs growled, and Warren screamed as Lucky went for his throat. Chyna and Leia grabbed his arms, and Aggie and Rex each had a leg.

The gun fell from his hands, and I picked it up. I helped Dixie into the passenger seat.

Warren Keller was writhing on the ground, with blood flowing from several open wounds.

I pulled out the gun and pointed it at him. For the life of me, I couldn't recall any of the Schutzhund commands, which I knew Lucky knew, to prevent him from ripping Warren Keller's throat off. "Lucky, come," I ordered.

Immediately, he backed off the injured man, but the dog did not take his eyes off his target for one second.

"Chyna. Leia. Off." I pointed to the RV, and the large poodles obeyed.

I scooped Aggie up with one hand and tossed her inside the RV. Rex barked a couple more times and then ran into the RV after Aggie. Finally, I ordered Lucky into the RV.

I stood there, holding a gun on Warren Keller, who had stopped screaming. I wasn't sure if he was dead or merely passed out from his wounds. However, I wasn't about to check to find out. I hurried around to the driver's side and climbed in. I closed and locked all the doors.

I looked for my cell phone to call Red, and that's when Warren Keller got up and started to beat on the window, leaving bloody smears on the glass.

I found Dixie's keys and started the RV. Then I put my foot on the gas and took off.

Chapter 27

"Dear God, I can't do this. I can't do this."

I heard a feeble voice say, "Yes, you can."

I looked over at Dixie, who was barely conscious. I knew my friend was in serious trouble and needed medical attention. "Hang on, Dixie." I pressed the gas harder and steered the RV down Lookout Mountain. Initially, I took the mountain at a slow pace. However, after a few blocks, I felt a jolt.

I glanced in the rearview mirror and saw a luxury SUV driven by a red-faced and furious Warren Keller ram into the back.

"Oh God, he's trying to kill us." I pressed down on the accelerator.

The road down the mountain was one lane of traffic in each direction. Those ascending were closest to the mountain, and the downhill travelers were in the outside lane. Fear made me drive as close to the mountain as possible until I was forced into the right lane by an approaching car. I gripped the steering wheel so hard my hands hurt. My heart raced, and I started to panic.

"Calm down, Lilly," I said. "You can do this. You have to do this."

Another jolt from Warren Keller from behind forced me to jerk the wheel to prevent us from careening over the side of the mountain. Terror at being killed by a maniac overrode my fear of driving down the mountain, and I pressed the pedal and sped up.

My hands were sweating, and that's when I remembered the Bluetooth on Dixie's RV. I pushed the button on the steering wheel. When I heard the familiar ding, I screamed, "Call Red Olson."

The voice repeated the command and then dialed the number. Red picked up on the third ring. "Hey, beautifu—"

"It's Warren Keller. He murdered Naomi and Dixon, and he's trying to kill Dixie and me."

Red flipped the switch that sent him into full-blown law-enforcement mode. "Where are you?"

"Driving Dixie's RV down Lookout Mountain."

Warren Keller drove alongside and made a sharp right turn to try and force the RV off the mountain.

I screamed.

"Lilly, hang on. I'm calling nine-one-one, and I'm on my way."

"I can't do this."

"Yes, you can. You're a strong woman, and you can do this. You're an excellent driver. Where's Dixie?"

I glanced over at my friend. "He drugged her."

"Then you're going to have to keep driving."

I bit my lip and pressed the gas a bit more. "I'm so scared."

"I know you're scared, but you can do this. You have to get down that mountain. You can't miss Stephanie and Joe's wedding. Think about Stephanie."

I could hear a car door slam and traffic noise and knew Red was on his way. "She said they want to move to Chattanooga. She wants to be close when they start their family.

"You don't want to miss the birth of your grandchild. Now pull yourself together and drive."

A picture of a chubby, curly-haired baby flashed into my mind, and I knew he was right. I had to do this. Suddenly, I was filled with rage. *How dare he?* In that instant, I knew I couldn't let Warren Keller destroy my happiness. I looked ahead and caught sight of a small turnabout where hikers often parked to take one of the hiking trails. It was a small area, and there was one car parked there. I could hear sirens in the distance.

I checked the rearview mirror and saw Warren Keller's SUV speeding up to ram me again. At the last moment, I swerved the RV and pulled aside. When Warren went to ram into the back of me, he missed and flew over the side of the mountain.

A few minutes later, a fireman banged on the side of the RV. "You okay?"

I was shaking so bad I couldn't speak. Eventually, he opened the door and stepped inside. "Are you okay?"

I nodded.

Dixie moaned from the passenger seat. "Help my friend. She's been drugged with diazepam."

The EMTs pulled Dixie out of the RV and got her into an ambulance.

I was still unable to move. Red pushed his way into the vehicle. "Thank God." He hugged me, but I was frozen. I couldn't let go of the steering wheel. I sat there crying and gripping that wheel like a life preserver.

Red crouched down. "Lilly, let go of the wheel."

I tried, but my brain couldn't get my fingers to move.

Red tried to pry my fingers off the wheel, but they were locked. He stepped out of the vehicle to get help. That's when Aggie walked up to my seat. She jumped up into my lap, stood on her hind legs, and licked my face.

After a few moments, I felt myself start to unfreeze, and I was able to release the steering wheel. I have no idea how long I sat there crying and hugging my dog, but it felt like years. Red returned and carried me out of the RV, though I was still clinging to Aggie.

He held me tight, and I could feel his body shake and the warm tears that flowed down his face.

He kissed my hair. "When this is over, I have a question I want to ask."

"My answer is yes."

He gazed into my eyes. "Are you sure?"

"When I was coming down that mountain and I thought of everything I'd miss if I . . . failed, I thought of my children and my future grandchildren, but mostly, I thought of you."

He pulled me close and kissed me.

Aggie wiggled her body between us, and Rex climbed on my lap. I looked around and saw Chyna, Leia, and Lucky sniffing the ground nearby. I thought of how these animals had protected me, and for the first time in my life, I knew what true, unconditional love felt like. I turned to Red. "Can you help me up?"

He looked surprised, but he stood and reached down and helped me to my feet. "The EMTs need to check you out, and then I'll follow you to the hospital."

I shook my head. "I don't need to go to the hospital."

"You're probably suffering from shock. You need to let the doctor decide if you're okay or not."

I sighed. "Okay, but you know what it will mean if I go to the hospital?"

He frowned. "What will it mean?"

"You'll have to explain to your family why I'm canceling the housewarming."

Epilogue

We moved the housewarming back one week, but no one seemed to mind. Despite being drugged, Dixie recovered quickly and was back to normal—apart from the fact that Beau, Chyna, and Leia weren't willing to leave her side for more than five minutes. However, with the new business to prepare for, she was happy for the extra support.

Monica Jill hadn't completely wrapped her mind around the fact that she was going to be having a baby. However, between B.J. and her husband, Zach, she was getting there. She swore she didn't know which one of the two of them was more excited. B.J. was enjoying buying baby clothes and had already bought more diapers and onesies than any infant could possibly use. Zach's frugal nature couldn't accept the high price of nursery furniture, so he was planning to build the round crib that Monica Jill wanted. All in all, she was adjusting to her new reality.

Stephanie missed her conference, but she and Joe decided to stay an extra week, which worked out perfectly. She and Theodore Jordan hit it off so well that he offered her a job at his firm. He had a small practice where he handled mostly civil rights complaints, which was right up her alley. Of course, Red promised to put in a good word for Joe at the TBI. Considering the Bureau was understaffed and Joe had an excellent record with the Lighthouse Dunes Police Department, it was an easy sell.

David's apartment was taking longer than originally planned to repair. Once the floors and walls were removed, other problems came to light, including electrical and plumbing issues. The project snowballed, and his unit wouldn't be habitable for months. He and Madison got to spend a lot more time together, which gave me hope for their future.

Red's family was wonderful. His mother and all of his sisters were loving and welcomed me with open arms. As an only child, I was a bit overwhelmed at times when everyone came together. However, it was also comforting to see the love the family had for each other. Even Aggie and Rex were getting more love, belly rubs, and treats, and were loving it.

During a moment when everyone was busy, I slipped inside and gazed out the kitchen window. Everyone was laughing, talking, and enjoying themselves. Linda Kay and Jacob from my work family were laughing with my friends from the dog club. Red, Stephanie, Joe, and David were joking with Red's family. Even the dogs were happily romping together and enjoying themselves.

Unlike my barren life in Indiana, my yard and my heart were full, and I was at peace. This was my happy place, and I was thankful, more than ever, for Miss Florrie for helping me to realize that happiness was possible. I wiped away a tear of joy and whispered, "Thank you."

Printed in the United States
by Baker & Taylor Publisher Services